Biography

Nathan Evans is a writer and performer based in London. Publishers of his poetry include Royal Society of Literature, Fourteen Poems, Broken Sleep and Manchester Metropolitan University; his debut collection *Threads*—a collaboration with photographer Justin David—was longlisted for the Polari First Book Prize 2017; his second collection CNUT is published by Inkandescent. Publishers of his short fiction include Queerlings and Muswell Press. His debut novella *One Last Song* was selected by iNewspaper as one of the best new LGBTQ+ books for Pride Month and was longlisted for the Polari Book Prize 2024.

Nathan's work in theatre and film has been funded by Arts Council England, toured with the British Council, archived by the British Film Institute, broadcast on Channel 4 and presented at venues including Royal Festival Hall and Royal Vauxhall Tavern. He produces BOLD Queer Poetry Soirée, and has hosted events for National Poetry Library, Charleston Small Wonder Festival and Stoke Newington Literary Festival; he teaches on the BA Creative Writing and English Literature at London Metropolitan University, and is editor at Inkandescent.

www.nathanevans.co.uk

Praise for *All the Young Queers*

'original, compelling and cleverly crafted'
JON RANSOM

'A wonderful collection of bildungsroman stories, full of vibrant characters finding their place in a jaded world. Evans beautifully captures the steep learning curve of each young protagonist—characters who must traverse religious, social, political and sexual dilemmas in order to discover who they really are. Evans is not afraid to play with voice and structure, making this a smart, insightful collection, where every story sparkles with rich, engaging prose and the perfect balance of humour and poignancy. All the Young Queers is an absolute joy to read!'
KATHY HOYLE

'An astonishingly accomplished range of stories, beautifully written, taking in everything from first love to chemsex, set in the recent past, among the hallowed walls of academia and even in other worlds. Tales steeped in nostalgia, politics and a groundswell of change. A masterful blending of periods, politics and formats, including stories written in text messages and court documents. I laughed, I cried, I nodded my head in recognition. I felt seen.'
IQBAL HUSSAIN

Praise for *One Last Song*

'An enchanting romance—funny, touching and inspiring'
STEPHEN FRY

'It's very funny, very touching and has the absolute ring of truth about it.
One can't but fall in love with these two more or less impossible people, as
they fall in love with each other.'
SIMON CALLOW

'Adored this book and couldn't put it down. An unapologetically queer
love story set in a care home. Touching. Heartwarming. Funny. Sad.
Beautifully drawn characters I wanted to spend more time with. It was
over too quickly for me. Joan and Jim, and their burgeoning relationship
will stay with me for a long time. I loved it.'
JONATHAN HARVEY

'One Last Song is a necessary love story, both profoundly moving and
profoundly optimistic. It will almost inevitably infiltrate your heart.'
MARTIN SHERMAN

'A warm, joyful and ingenious tale of gay love
from the UK's Armistead Maupin.'
JOELLE TAYLOR

'When we forget our gay elders and the radical queer people who lived so
we could fly, we forget ourselves. Nathan Evans has not just remembered
these elder angels, he has painted them with humour, love, truth and
glory. This is a gem of a novella.'
ADAM ZMITH

'One Last Song is a beautiful, smouldering, hilarious and sparkling
testament to queer intimacy and the revolutionary potency of queer
creative activism. Every page filled my heart with Pride.'
DAN GLASS

Inkandescent

First published by Inkandescent, 2025
Text Copyright © 2025 Nathan Evans
Cover Design Copyright © 2025 Justin David
Artwork Copyright © 2025 Nathan Evans

A CIP record for this book is available from the British Library

Printed in the UK by Short Run Press, Exeter

MIX
Paper | Supporting
responsible forestry
FSC® C014540

ISBN 978-1-912620-31-9 (paperback)
ISBN 978-1-912620-32-6 (ebook)

1 3 5 7 9 10 8 6 4 2

www.inkandescent.co.uk

for Justin
for encouraging me to try my hand at fiction
for everything

Also by Nathan Evans

poetry
Threads
CNUT

fiction
One Last Song

All the YOUNG QUEERS 16-24 YEARS

Nathan Evans

Inkandescent
celebrating diversity

Contents

16

Glass House

'Shouldn't have that on this time of morning,' Mum says as she barges in without knocking. 'Cost a fortune.'

'Bank holiday,' I say. 'Cheap rate.' And I lean in to cover the computer screen as she strides across the room to fling the airing cupboard open. *So annoying.* When they built the extension, the boiler ended up in my room for some reason. 'What time you leaving?'

'Soon. First race is at ten.'

She grabs three pairs of freshly-aired trainers—three different colours, same stupid tick—then races off downstairs again, calling, 'You finished those sandwiches, Ian?'

She's left the door wide open. I sigh and shut it after her, then go back to the website for a last-minute check.

Is it today?

Yes. May the first.

And do I know where?

Yes. London A-to-Z. Pocket of my army trousers.

Turn off the computer. Go downstairs. In the living room, David is watching television—wearing matching trainers and tracksuit bottoms. In the dining room, Mum is torturing her hair before the mirror. In the kitchen, Dad is spreading sliced wheatgerm with margarine. He has to shout over the drone of Mum's dryer.

'What time's your train?'

'Quarter to ten.'

'Want a lift to the station?'

'It's alright. I'll walk.'

I sit eating cereal, drinking tea as sandwiches are packed into boxes, boxes into bags, and bags into the boot of the car.

At the front door, Mum hands me a fiver.

'Get yourself a McDonald's.'

'No thanks.'

'Something *vegetarian* then!'

In the driver's seat, Dad starts the engine. In the backseat, David sticks out his tongue. In the passenger seat, Mum belts up and belts out, 'You be back by seven!'

'Yes, Mum!'

'And don't do anything I wouldn't!'

Her door slams shut, and they're off. Up the road and round the corner. I hold my breath and listen for the last of the motor. Then grab my bag and head out the back door.

The greenhouse is at the top of the garden. Dad grows cucumbers in summer, but it's mine the rest of the year. I open my bag and, one by one, place the pots inside.

I'm ready to leave by nine-fifteen. Make a last check I've got everything.

Money. Key. Pen. Water, sandwiches. Ventolin.

I've never been to London on my own. But now I'm sixteen, Mum says I can. I *have* been with school to see the National Gallery. That's where she thinks I'm going today.

Westminster station is surrounded by police. I try not to make eye contact as I exit, and join the crowd *reclaiming the street*.

Some are carrying flowers. One or two with wheelbarrows. A woman wearing face paint hands me a leaflet. *Guerrilla Gardening! Mayday Action!* I'm in the right place, then. The leaflet explains that—should the police get me—I have *the right to remain silent and should consult a lawyer before saying anything.*

There's a number at the bottom.

Look up. See a woman climbing a lamp post. And over there, there's another one. Something is swinging on a rope between them. It's a banner. It says *Let London Sprout.*

Fucking brilliant.

Someone's put a maypole up. Kids are dancing round it. Someone else has put grass down in the street. They're having a picnic. And there's a strip of grass on this statue's bald head. Looks like a mohican.

Fucking brilliant.

Wander to the centre of the square. The earth feels lumpy beneath my feet. They must have laid turf in the night. But now, they're digging it up and putting in plants. I try not to tread on any of them. Some look like they've already been stood on. Others are wilting in the sunshine. The website said *bring water.* Looks like no one bothered. I brought two litres. This bag's killing my shoulder.

I stop in the corner and put it down. I look around. The website said *form groups.* I kind of assumed it would just happen.

Realise I don't know anyone.

'Window shoppers not welcome.'

He's about the same age as me. Bit older maybe. Mohican, like the statue—except his is blue—and a ring through his eyebrow. He's pulling up flowers with his fingernails.

'Sorry, what did you say again?'

'Fuck off or give us a hand.'

He turns back to his tulips. I find my fork and join him in the flowerbed.

'I'm Jason.'

He nods. 'Bod.'

I've never met a Bod before. 'Why are you pulling up plants that're already here?'

'Liberating them.'

'What from?'

'Borders are a form of fascist oppression.'

He starts ripping up grass—with only his fingers, hard work. I lend him the fork, then carefully manoeuvre a cutting between my bag's zipper.

'Does it matter where?'

'You mean you don't have permission?'

'Do I have to get...'

He laughs. 'Wherever you like, man.'

Feel stupid. Start digging. 'What are they filming?'

'Who?'

'The policemen.' They've got cameras—those little digital ones.

'Us. Fucking perverts.'

I hide behind my hair. Give my plants water. Try to make them stand straighter. Bod has finished. His are lopsided.

'Very nice,' he says. 'You want some of this?'

I had a joint once. When Trevor's parents went away the weekend. Didn't really do anything. I'm asthmatic. I'm not very good at inhaling.

'Alright then.' I check no-one's looking and take it from him.

'Been on one of these before?' He lolls back. And his *System of a Down* t-shirt rides up.

'No. You?' I try not to look at his belly fluff.

'Yeah. See those riots last year? I was there. Fucking give the pigs what for.'

I try not to cough.

How embarrassing.

I try again.

I'm laid back on the grass watching clouds floating past when I notice a woman stood over us.

'Give us a drag, Bod.'

She's older than we are, hair laced with shells and silver. Bod passes the joint over.

'Jason, this is Maya.'

She smiles in my direction. 'Some great stuff going down.'

'Mm.' I seem to be grinning.

'You come on your own?'

'Mm.' I seem to be unable to formulate a sentence.

'Aw...'

I turn to the sky again. Try to focus on something but the clouds keep moving.

'Fucking brilliant man!' A guy with blond dreads looms into vision. 'Someone smashed the McDonald's in.'

Bod says, 'Where?'

Dreads says, 'Trafalgar Square.'

Bod says, 'I'm there.'

He jumps up. 'Coming?'

I realise he's looking in my direction.

There's this statue on which someone has written *men's toilet*. Bod laughs and takes advantage. We notice some policemen and run. I try not to notice Bod's dick, still dangling from his zip. He shouts, 'Fucking pigs!'

There's this sea of heads and Nelson's Column in the middle. Bod tries to push through but there's too many people. 'Fuck this.' He pulls me into a side street.

There's this row of police vans and policemen piling from them. They're wearing masks. They've got shields on their arms.

And then they're stood between us and Trafalgar Square. On this side are protesters. On that side are protesters. The police keep piling in, hundreds of them, forming lines behind the front one. I don't understand what's going on.

'Why do they have to spoil everything?'

'Because they're fucking pigs.'

When we work out the police are letting in tourists, we squeeze past, pretending not to speak English. Inside the square, it's emptier than expected. And strangely silent.

There's the police.

And then there's us.

Now what?

I notice the sun has gone in. Then I hear something smashing and a woman screaming. She's got a baby in a pushchair. She shouts, 'Keep together, keep together!' as her other kids run after her.

Bod's laughing. He's got a bottle in his hand. He says, 'Your turn.'

His eyes are blue as his mohican. My heart stops beating. I look down to see my hand take the bottle from him.

I've never been good at throwing. I don't expect to hit anything.

The policeman just keeps staring, staring as splinters fall around him.

I stand waiting for the earth to open. It doesn't.

Fucking pig.

I'm addicted.

When the police start moving in, we run—back out the way we came.

Bod pulls up out of breath. 'I need a drink.'

I offer what's left of my water. He shakes his head.

'There's this party at Maya's—you wanna come?'

'Should be going—said I'd be home by seven.'

Fuck. Did I really just say that?

His eyebrow ring rides up a bit.

Now I've really blown it.

'You got a number? Be back in London again soon.'

Not got any paper, so he writes on my travel card. I say I'll call him maybe next week, and watch his blue fin dipping in and out of vision along the crowded street.

When I get home, they're all watching television.

Dad says, 'Didn't want a lift then?'

And Mum, 'Best put your own dinner in the oven.'

Marks and Spencer's *vegetarian* lasagne. Still eating when she calls through to the kitchen. 'You see this, Jason? Been a riot in London.'

I hear the reporter from outside the living room door, '... defacing a statue of Winston Churchill before proceeding up Whitehall...'

Mum says, 'Innit terrible?'

My heart beats triple-time as I step in.

'...the Cenotaph was desecrated...'

I loiter behind the sofa, staring at the screen over their shoulders.

'...a branch of McDonald's vandalised...'

It's not the same protest at all. There's no plants. No maypoles. Just pixelated pictures of smashed windows.

'...the National Gallery forced to shut...'

Mum says, 'Isn't that where you went?'

'Must have been after I left.'

But the screen contradicts. Because there I am. And there's the bottle, leaving my hand.

David stares from his armchair. The silence from the sofa lasts forever. Or at least until broken by the news reporter.

'...police are requesting that viewers who recognise any protesters please call the number now appearing on your screen...'

She says, 'Pass me the phone, Ian.'

'What're you doing?'

'That wasn't why you were let go to London.'

'But, but...' My hard drive is struggling to start up. 'It wasn't like that!'

'Like what?'

'It was the police's fault.'

Her eyebrows knit, like she can't compute this. 'Don't be ridiculous!'

'Everything was fine until they came along.'

She says, 'Ian, will you pass me the phone.'

He says, 'Your great-grandfather died in that war.'

'What war?'

'World War Two. They teach you anything at that school?'

'So?' I centimetre towards the door.

'The Cenotaph. Do you know what it's for? It's for all the soldiers who died, yeah? And without those men, you wouldn't even be here,' he says as he picks up the receiver.

I run. Out the front door and onto the street. He runs after. 'Get back here!'

He's faster. But he's wearing slippers. One of them falls off. He has to stop.

I stop around the corner.

Fuck! What if he comes after me in the car?

Keep running. Can't see for sweating.

What am I gonna do?

My fingers find a solution, as they scramble in my pocket for a tissue.

07700900312.

Take a breath. Insert ten pence.

I'm in the call box outside Chatham station. Checking out the window that Dad isn't coming. Take travelcard from pocket. Dial number on it. Look at my watch. There's a train in two minutes. If he answers now I might just catch it.

'Hello?' It's him.

'Bod, it's Jason. I was wondering…'

He's hung up.

No. It's a fucking mobile. The fucking money's run out.

No change. No time to get more. Got to get the train now or wait another hour.

Arrive on the platform as the train's pulling in. No time for the ticket machine. All the way back to London, I'm praying the inspector doesn't come.

He doesn't.

Victoria Station. My last tenner. Buy a Mars bar. Line up the change on top of the phone.

'Hello?'

'Bod, it's Jason.'

'Who?'

'Jason!' Have to shout. Music blaring in the background. 'We met this afternoon?'

'Yeah, man. How's it going?'

'Alright, I…' *Another twenty.* 'You at the party?'

'Fuck man. Don't know *where* I am.'
Another ten. 'You said I could come?'
'Do what you like, man.'
And another one. 'Well, where is it then?'
'Brixton.'
Seconds left. 'But what's the address?'
'Acre Lane.'
It's beeping. 'What number?'
'Fifty-nine.'

Brixton is on the Victoria line. Still got my travel card. Still got my A to Z. Pocket of my army trousers. On the underground, I memorise directions. *Left out the station, right at the junction.*
  Brixton is full-on. Busy as the protest this morning.
Left out the station.
And like this morning, I keep my head down.
Right at the junction.
Acre Lane. *Can hear the music.* Number fifty-nine.
Front garden's a state. Front door's flaking paint. I knock on it. Nothing.
Knock louder.
It opens.
'Hello, dear.' It's Maya. 'Wasn't expecting to see you here.'
'Neither was I.' Feel blood draining into my DMs. 'Is it okay?'
'Course!' She folds me into the tie-dye she's wearing. 'Come in.'
Mum would say she *needs a good washing*. 'You want a beer or something?'
I take the bottle from her hand.
Not throwing this one.

'Bod!'

He's sprawling in a pile of cushions. I have to dodge dancers to reach him.

'Bod?'

He looks up. His eyes take a long, long moment to focus. He nods.

I sit down. Justify my presence in the room.

'Had to come.'

He's rolling another joint. Doesn't look like he needs it.

'My parents went ballistic—you see it?'

He lights up. 'What?'

'The news report.'

'No man. You give us a blowback?'

'A what?'

He laughs. 'Come closer and I'll show ya...'

His eyes are rings of blue, floating in pink pools. They point in my direction but he isn't really looking, isn't really seeing.

'Fucking brilliant.'

The weed is all he's taking in.

Suddenly the music stops. The guy with dreads who came running over in the square has turned on the television in the corner. It's a repeat of the report from earlier. And there I am. I made it to the headlines.

'Let me shake your hand, man.' A big guy with a beard slaps me on the back and crushes my fingers. 'Welcome to the revolution.'

Someone cheers. I smile. Turn to Bod. Bod isn't interested.

'Totally fucking misrepresented.' Dreads is pacing. 'They twist and turn everything to their own ends.'

'That's because we're a threat,' says a guy with a hat. 'They feel threatened because we see through their fucking system.'

'Too fucking right, man.'

For the first time, they're showing pictures of the Parliament Square planting. I ask, 'Who put the grass down?'

'Fucking Parliament, I expect.'

'But it was lumpy.'

'Can't trust that lot to do anything properly.'

I frown. 'We were digging up real grass then?'

Beard laughs. 'Wish it had been.'

'But…' I hesitate. 'What's the point in that?'

He pulls a packet of Marlboro from his pocket. 'It's symbolic.'

'Of what?'

'What do you mean?'

'It can't just be symbolic. It's got to be symbolic of something.'

Not sure where this is coming from.

'Fucking lost me, man.'

'Well, what about the Cenotaph?' They're showing it on TV. 'Isn't that symbolic?'

Dreads grabs for his crotch. 'It is now I've anointed it.'

I avert my eyes to the floor. He's got Nike trainers. Same colour Dad wears.

And when I open my mouth, Dad's voice comes out. 'My great-grandfather died in that war.'

Hat swigs from a can of Coca-Cola. 'Listen man, I'm sorry about your grandpa and everything, but you gotta understand that war is just another form of capitalist exploitation.'

'Without that war, we'd be living in a world ruled over by Hitler.'

Dreads says, 'Couldn't be any worse than Tony Blair.'

'Don't be ridiculous.'

And now my mother.

'Who let this little cunt in here?'

Bod says, 'Fucking followed me here. Fucking queer.'

The room goes silent. I sit frozen. Daren't turn my head in either direction. In the corner of one eye, I see bastard Bod. His blue mohican bobbing as the beat drops back in. *Bastard Bod. Bod the Bastard.* Bobbing, bobbing.

I get up and go out to the garden. Down to the bottom. It's dark and it's quiet. Smells like my greenhouse. Take deep breaths. Take it out on a tree trunk. Imagine it's him.

And then I'm crying.

'You alright?'

It's Maya. Can just about see her.

'I'm fine.' Hope she can't make out my tears.

'Why don't you go home, dear?' She squeezes my shoulder. 'Bit out of your depth here.'

'I can't...' And then I'm tearing up again and telling her how my parents have turned me in. She takes me in her arms, and I don't even care about her smelling.

'Why don't you let me ring them and tell them you're safe and you'll see them in the morning?'

'But where will I sleep, then?'

'Well, it's a nice evening...'

Don't know what she says to them. I stay out in the garden. She brings blankets and cushions. I lay looking at the moon.

I've never slept outside before. Worry about bugs in my ears. Turn and press one of them into a cushion. But I'm facing the house, then. At this distance, the dancers are out of sync with the beats. A blue fin bobs between them, like they're reefs.

I turn to the moon again. There's even come stars in the background.

27

Who says you can't see them in London?
In the foreground, leaves rustling. In my ribs, roots prodding.
Inside, something growing.

In the morning, everything's aching. I shake out my limbs, shake blankets and cushions. The back door is open. People crashed everywhere. I pick my way between them, hoping he's not there.

He isn't.

I want to say goodbye to Maya but don't know where to find her. I want to leave a note but don't have any paper. Still got the pen in my pocket. So I leave yesterday's ticket on the doormat—Bod's number scribbled out and, in tiny letters, the tinniest of thank you notes.

Brixton is still full-on. Some selling salvation over sound-systems. Some seeking sacrament in storefronts. And some begging *a little change* outside the station.

I take the underground to Victoria. But then swap to the Circle Line. I can't resist the two stops to Westminster again.

The statues have been boarded and cleaners have moved in. The grass is in ruins. One or two sad stick constructions, plants wilting over them. I walk round and around the square. When the policeman isn't looking, I jump the barrier. Over to the corner. There's one of them still there. I dig it out with my fingers.

All the way home, it prickles in the pocket of my trousers.

My parents are pleased to see me—I am sentenced to indefinite imprisonment and two weeks hard labour at the kitchen sink. But I still have my kingdom at the top of the garden, and starting with the salvaged cutting, I do some much-needed repotting.

When a plant becomes pot-bound, the pot needs removing. The roots should be loosened, then replanted in something with room for them to grow in.

When I'm done, they're in rows—sorted by size and neatly labelled.

I've got twenty-four species of cacti and succulent. On earth, there are four thousand.

Five thousand stars are visible from the earth at any one time. Or so they told us in science… How many did I see last night from Maya's garden?

Looking at the sky today, I see the panes of the greenhouse are actually grey. They make everything outside them seem fuzzy.

The clouds, racing.

The trainers on the rotary line, airing. Three pairs, three colours—red, blue, green. Same stupid tick on all of them.

The thing with throwing is, you got to aim at the right thing. And like I'm at one of those side-stalls at a fairground, I wait with a weight in my hand for the targets to swing round.

Here they are—six chances of winning. I take a big breath of thick greenhouse air.

And then the world isn't fuzzy anymore. The air is thinner. The door is banging for want of a brick to prop it open.

In Classics, they told us Nike is the goddess of victory. Five pieces of her footwear are still spinning. But one of them is lying in a bed of broken illusions.

And one tiny victory is mine.

17

The Magic Machine

Once upon a time in a world like this one, there lived a young worldling called Daimon who worked all day and every day in a factory as wide as a country and filled to the brim with other young worldlings like him, working all day and every day to make magic machines.

The possessor of such a machine would have magical powers at the touch of their fingers: the power to conjure visions as if from the air, the power to speak with spirits who were not there, to ask any question and be given the answer, and to never be lost or lonely or unhappy. Daimon wanted more than anything to be happy again, to smile and feel sunshine on his skin—so he went on working all and every day, saving every cent he could save from his minimal wage, in the hope that one day he could buy a machine. And become a magician.

He kept the savings in a box beneath his mattress. The factory dormitories were so crowded that there weren't enough beds to go round, and so Daimon shared with Yann. Every evening he would fall exhausted into Yann's firm arms and hear Yann's firm voice at his ear—whispering how he didn't think it fair that the magicians who ruled over the factory should have all the power and all the money and all the magic things. And Daimon would kiss Yann to quiet him—for the magicians were always listening.

Daimon and Yann and all the other young worldlings were summoned early each morning; they all worked all day without stopping. Their job was to polish the screens of magic machines. The screens were made of a crystal so powerful it could kill, so the polishers wore special clothing, ugly and ill-fitting, to protect them from the crystal dust which flew all about them.

The magicians also wore special clothing, but theirs was sleek and shining. As was the voice of the magician in charge of the polishing when, one morning, she descended through the glass ceiling to address her polishing team: she, Volta, was upgrading Zora, her *hardest worker*. And she raised Zora magically through the air, so high she disappeared. Into the unknown of the upper echelons. And although he would never have admitted it to Yann, Daimon was jealous—for Zora would be given her own machine there.

Then Volta's voice sharpened as she told those remaining that more machines must be made in less time. And if they didn't meet this new target she'd set, then they knew what would happen: they'd be flung from the factory into the world which lay beyond. A world as hard as a sun-shrivelled orange. And some dry, desperate worldling would be only too happy to replace them.

The polishers' hearts sank to the floor, for how could they work any harder or faster? But none dared speak anything of what they were thinking, none except Yann.

'It cannot be done!'

Yann's voice rang across the machine room and back from the glass ceiling. Daimon sat frozen as his friend stood beside him and told the magician that if they were to polish any harder or faster the crystal might well catch fire, and why would they take that risk when all profits from increased production would go to the magicians and not to them?

He looked to Daimon to support him; Daimon could feel Yann's eyes upon him, and he could see Volta eyeing up both of them. Daimon was seventeen then, but could still recall being ten—and the dry, desperate hands with which his mother had waved goodbye to him at the factory entrance. So Daimon looked down and said nothing. And when he looked up again, a swarm of sorcerers were spiriting Yann away from him.

The last look Yann gave him stayed burnt on Daimon's brain. That evening, he lay in bed without Yann beside him and without sleeping—if he closed his eyes, he saw only Yann's disappointment. And the next day, he worked harder and faster at his polishing—as if trying to scrub that disappointment from his brain. And so it went on: every night, unsleeping; every day, harder and faster, smoothing and shining.

He did not see the warning meter flashing: he saw only the world turning white around him. He felt himself flying, then falling; he smelt himself burning and bleeding; he heard himself screaming. And the echo of that scream in every nerve ending drowned the sound of Volta's voice telling him how he would pay for the damage he'd done as she loomed over him and glitter dust snowed all about him, onto his skin, or where his skin had been, and even as it cooled him, Daimon knew it could kill him.

And then there was nothing, not even pain. The world was cool and green, as his mother had told him it had once been. And his mother was beside him—telling him, as she had when he was young, that one day, *one day*, he would become a magician.

When his eyes opened, Daimon had no way of knowing if it was the same day or a new one. Or whether he was the same person or a new one. His last recollection was of the explosion, which had whited out everything. Now, he was staring at a white ceiling; it had the familiar factory lighting that never dimmed, be it daytime or nighttime, but now it seemed brighter than it had ever been. And there was a sharpness to everything: he could follow the fine lines of cracks, as though reading a map. A map might tell him where he now found himself lying. Not on the factory floor, or in the dormitory, he was sure. He could hear no machinery, no snoring. But he could hear, with precision, every nuance of silence. And footsteps approaching, in the distance.

Daimon sat up, with an energy that surprised him. Although not as much as the sight of his own skin. It had regrown, but not as it had previously been: it now shone, sparkled in the light as he moved. Like glitter, like crystal.

He heard a portal opening, felt the temperature dropping. And a shadow fell on his glittering skin; Volta was stood over him, shining clothing accentuating her own dull complexion.

'Well, this is most interesting.' She looked him up and down, smiling, then spoke into her magic machine: 'Put me through to Master Maling.'

Before his head could catch up with him, Daimon found himself in motion—leaping from the bed in which he'd woken, feet—bare as the rest of him—landing on cold floor, then running—faster than ever before—from that room, white and austere, past Volta and through the door.

But outside in the corridor he found more sorcerers, advancing upon him.

'And just where do you think you're going?' Volta's voice goaded Daimon.

He was trapped between the magicians ahead and the magician behind him. He stopped running and again, his body knew what needed to be done.

His sharp eyes spotted the airduct above him. And he leapt—away from the ground and up, up towards the duct—

almost as if he were weightless. And then, as if he weighed almost nothing, he lifted himself into the air vent.

It took only a moment for his super-vision to adjust to the darkness within. And he allowed himself but a moment to take stock of what he had done, of what he may have become. Because his super-hearing told him the magicians were attempting to clamber up after him.

He sped on—sliding and slipping through spaces too small for any sorcerer to pass through. And so he lost them, and found his way through the ducts—turning and twisting through the guts of the factory until they bore him once more into the world beyond the factory doors.

He felt the heat before he saw the sunlight at the end of the air vent. He found himself squinting out on a sea of shimmering sand. And when he leapt the long leap down to the ground, the grains beneath his feet were burning.

The air duct had delivered Daimon right beside the factory entrance. It had been seven years since he'd passed through those dark doors, clutching his moneybox, now left behind beneath his mattress. His mother had handed the box to him with the instruction to *work hard, save wisely, and be happy*. At all but the first he had failed miserably.

He was startled from his recollection by the sound of locks turning. Perhaps realising where the duct might lead him, the magicians had taken a more conventional route to pursue Daimon, and now the doors were opening. Without thinking, Daimon sped onwards over orange sands.

His velocity was exhilarating, the power in his limbs intoxicating; only once did he glance back towards the factory—piled to the sky like boxes, each one smaller than that on which it rested—and capped with a crystal pinnacle, which pierced the cadmium sunset.

And in the peak of that pinnacle, Master Magician Maling—who drew the world's juices to him as a blister draws blood beneath skin—saw the shimmering trail Daimon left behind him and knew the time was coming.

Daimon's exhilaration did not last long: he soon came down to earth, or somewhere not unlike it. Things outside the factory were worse, far worse than he remembered—the world now one great desert. He sped, then strode, then stumbled up dunes and down them, as the savage sun sank and rose again—once, then twice, then three times. Daimon could clearly see every horizon, be it daytime or night-time, but no other living thing ever entered his super-vision. And what good were superpowers to him when he still needed to eat and drink like any ordinary human?

On the fourth evening, he found his vision failing—for the factory that had been behind him was once again before him, its pinnacle rising above the horizon. And then, his whole body was failing him: he surrendered to sand, in exhaustion. Regret overcame him. *Why had he not seen the meter's warning? Why had he said nothing as Yann was taken from him?*

In his head, he could hear Yann, sweet Yann, but when he raised his head, he heard *sweet nothing*. Yet resting his head again, there was Yann—like he was whispering to Daimon, like he was somehow in the sand beneath him.

In delirium, Daimon began digging. And with every last scrap of super-strength, he kept digging his way towards the sound of Yann singing—*he was singing!* But always that bit further beneath and beyond—Daimon despaired of ever reaching him. Then the earth began caving in, and Daimon found himself falling—into Yann's firm arms again.

He was wrestled to the ground, or to the underground—

he'd fallen to the floor of some subterranean cavern where a figure was firmly pinning him down. Had Daimon not heard Yann's singing, he would barely have known his old friend—whose skin was soiled and stinking. And Yann's eyes showed no recognition of Daimon—in his shining new skin.

'Yann, I'm so sorry!' Daimon let fly the apology he'd feared might never be given. 'I'll never, ever disappoint you again.'

'Daimon?' Yann released his grip on him.

Then Daimon told Yann everything—about the explosion, his extraordinary transformation and escape from the magicians. And Yann told Daimon off for not seconding him that morning when he'd stood up to the magicians. Daimon apologised again, giving his reasons; Yann forgave him then, and embraced him.

Yann shared some meagre morsels with Daimon, which began to revive him. Yann also shared his story: after his ejection from the factory, he too had spent days wandering beneath the searing sun, searching for sustenance. And he too had stumbled upon this cavern—where he'd found other factory rejects eking out an existence. He'd been invited to join their commune and, on the evening Daimon had stumbled across him, it was his turn to keep watch for them—he'd been singing to stop himself from sleeping.

Lulled by Yann's voice, Daimon could feel his own eyes grow heavy with sleep—for what felt like the first time in weeks. He turned to Yann to kiss him goodnight, and it was then that another extraordinary thing happened: as lip met lip, the shimmer slipped from Daimon into Yann; he too, became a glittering being.

And that night, in their togetherness, Daimon felt the happiest he could ever remember feeling.

He woke to find the sun piercing the mouth of the cavern

and Yann's arms no longer around him. Daimon called out for Yann, but only his own voice echoed back at him.

Had he imagined everything?

Then the sound of other voices reached his super-hearing. One of them was Yann's. And as Daimon descended towards those voices, into the darkness of the cavern, he felt his spirits plummeting. For there, ahead, two lights were shining: Yann and a woman beside him.

And like Yann's own, her skin was shimmering.

'Welcome to the commune,' said the woman. 'Here we share everything.'

Daimon's happiness and Daimon's uniqueness had both been short-lived: though he would never have admitted it to Yann, Daimon would've preferred to keep both his power and his lover to himself alone.

There were six in the commune, seven including Daimon. And soon they all became glittering beings—with super-vision and super-hearing, but whose bellies needed filling like any other human. One evening, they were sharing the most meagre of meals—roots with traces of moisture still in them, dug from the earth about them. Daimon was sat, as usual, on the perimeter of their circle. And conversation turned, again, to magicians.

Raine fed Yann his cue-line from her place beside him. 'What is to be done?'

'We must bring down Maling!' Yann did not disappoint, at least not Raine.

Perhaps Daimon's disappointment in Yann was some form of retribution, heavenly or human, but Daimon remained determined to never let his friend down again. An idea came to him—a chance to impress Yann and seize sole control of his affections.

'I can lead you to Maling,' he announced to the cavern.

And so, on a night with no moonbeams to betray their sparkling skins, Daimon led the band of factory rejects back to the factory doorstep, then up into the duct beside it. He led them back through the factory's guts, past the corridor where—he told the others—he'd outwitted the sorcerers. Past the room where he'd first discovered his special powers—which, he reminded them, had allowed them all to gain them. And past the boys' dorm.

How strange it seemed to return a free being to the place where he'd been enslaved for so long and to look down on two new dull-skinned worldlings in the bed he'd shared with Yann.

Yann had perhaps been feeling the same thing; he slipped an arm around Daimon.

'You know, I still love you,' he whispered, before pausing. 'But I need to love others too.'

'So, this is the boy's dorm.' Raine was there to ruin the moment. 'I always dreamt of breaking in.'

'Well, now's your chance.' Daimon all but pushed her from the vent. 'Power to the people!'

'Yann, I still love you,' Raine called up from the dormitory below. 'But I need to love others too.'

As she set about spreading her shimmer amongst the men, Yann didn't look to be enjoying the taste of his own medicine; Daimon couldn't help smiling.

'Best leave her to it, then.'

As he led what remained of the band onwards and upwards towards Maling, Daimon's sense of direction was unerring, despite navigating a part of the duct system he'd never before been in. His powers, it seemed, were guiding him.

When they passed another air vent, Daimon brought them

to a halt to peer through it. Beneath them ranged machines—row upon row of them, magicians bowed before them, conjuring visions. Daimon knew then he had gained those upper echelons he'd dreamt so long of inhabiting, and that the glass ceiling must now be beneath them—though, strangely, they had not passed *through* anything.

Even stranger, when Daimon spotted Zora among the magicians—machine to ear, speaking with spirits who were not there—Volta's favoured worker looked more miserable than ever.

'Poor things,' said Yann, beside him. 'To be so enslaved by machines.'

Yann did seem to be right: every time a machine rang, a magician sped to serve it. But Daimon could not let go his illusions just yet. There must be more to magic—he *had* to believe that—and he *had* to discover what. The answer, he felt sure, would be found up above.

'Race you to the top.'

Daimon tugged at Yann's arm and—leaving the remaining rejects to disempower their former oppressors by whichever means they chose—the two of them continued alone.

Up and up and up. Daimon almost wished the ascent would never stop, so happy was he to have Yann to himself again. But finally, they emerged from the darkness of the duct into the vertiginous brightness of a crystalline palace.

The great shining summit that topped the factory and could be seen for miles around seemed, at close hand, to be built from light beams alone. And through those beams they could see the land below them—unravelling like the rind of an orange into an indigo ocean.

A voice spoke above them, sibilant as an infant:

'I'm afraid the gardens aren't much to look at, at the moment.'

The voice chilled Daimon. And for some reason, thrilled him.

At the peak of the pinnacle, where the beams converged, a shrunken and decrepit worldling was cradled. 'You must be Daimon,' the voice said, with amusement. 'And may I compliment you on your glowing complexion.' The figure was descending, magically, towards them.

'Who are you?' As usual, Yann had taken it upon himself to speak for Daimon.

'I'll give you a guess: it starts with an M.'

Yann scoffed. '*You* are the Master Magician?'

'Magic is illusion merely.' The voice was full of ennui. 'It exists only in the minds of those who wish to believe.'

Yann did not understand. 'Well, if you are Maling,' he proclaimed, 'then we must inform you that the factory is under new management.'

'Yes, I heard you've been spreading yourselves about.'

'And you have two options: abdicate or die!'

'Darling…' A wet chuckle emerged from the cradle, which was now almost at their level. 'In order to kill me, you would have first to kill the machine. And to kill the machine you must kill every worldling—for each one of them carry its mechanics within.'

Maling arrived before them, cadaverous and repellent.

'Though all except we three are as good as dead already.'

Daimon grabbed Yann's hand as the floor beneath their feet turned transparent and the crystal pinnacle began rising—a giant magic machine—away from the factory it had rested upon and up into the heavens.

'What good is a glittering skin, when there is nothing to feed the body within?' Maling's voice now grew more grandiloquent. 'It is but a gilded husk. Just as this planet is now a husk. The last of its essences are powering our take-off.'

'But *where* are you taking us?' Daimon's voice, found at last, shook as he spoke.

'That depends very much on what you do next.' Maling's eyes, like black holes, focused on Daimon, and Daimon alone. 'You, young man, have something I need and I… have *everything* you want.'

And again, Daimon felt that cool thrill.

'I, the mighty Maling, have harnessed all *about* me the powers of this planet. But you, a lowly worldling, have harnessed them *within*.' With a skeletal hand, he signalled Daimon's shimmering skin. 'Of course, you have little idea what to do with them—some heightened sensory experience, some superior athleticism—amateurs!' He made a dismissive gesture. 'What you need is a mentor, a master, to show you your *true* magic power—that's why I guided you here.'

Daimon felt his stomach tighten, like its contents had frozen.

'Oh yes, my darling, I've been tracking *you* for some time.' Maling's smile was sickening. 'So what do you say, then? You share your powers, and I shall share mine.'

Daimon's mind was an explosion of questions. *Didn't he want, more than anything, to become a magician? But hadn't Maling said that magic was illusion? And hadn't Daimon seen that himself in the upper echelons? But how did that explain the powers he now had within him? Could he become a truly powerful magician, if only he could learn how to use them?*

In that moment of hesitation and temptation, Maling extended his hand in slow-motion.

But Yann tightened *his* hand. 'No, Daimon!'

And Daimon had promised to never disappoint Yann again.

'I thought you shared everything?' Maling turned his dark eyes on Yann. 'Or is that only with pretty young worldlings called Raine?'

Daimon felt again his disappointment in Yann, and he felt Yann's grip loosen.

Maling's eyes turned back upon Daimon. 'You understand me, don't you, darling?'

And then the moneybox Daimon's mother had given him was magically in Maling's hand. Seeing it, Daimon remembered the advice she'd given with it; happiness had remained elusive.

'I've been saving this for you.' Maling shook the box to and fro—it sounded almost full. 'I may even have added a coin or two.'

The rattling was hypnotic. Daimon shivered with a coldness that was almost ecstatic.

'Take it, darling Daimon. Take *everything* I'm offering.'

Spellbound, Daimon slipped his hand from Yann's and reached towards Maling's.

'Not so quick.' The magician withdrew the box. 'First, a little kiss.'

Untranced, Daimon shrank back at the grotesqueness of this request.

'Now dearest, I know I'm not looking my best.' Maling looked affronted. 'A kiss of life is all that's needed. A new lease—for both of us.'

'Don't!' cried Yann.

He was grabbing again for Daimon when the floor dissolved beneath him, and suddenly Yann was falling—falling as fast as the machine was rising.

'Yann!'

Daimon was powerless to prevent it—even if he had the power within him, he knew not how to channel it. In moments, Yann was beyond the range of even Daimon's super-vision.

He had only ever wanted the love of one man, and now that man was gone.

Maling sighed feebly. 'Honestly darling, I have no idea what you saw in that one—but if you would like to join him, I can let you out at your convenience.'

Maling rattled the moneybox again, drawing Daimon's attention.

'Alternatively, there's a position going—*mastress* of a new planet—lovely spot, just a few galaxies off.'

Daimon looked down at the box in Maling's talons; it had lost all meaning, now he had lost Yann. And Daimon blamed himself for letting go of him.

'But you do need to hurry up and make a decision—we'll be leaving *this* world at any moment.' Maling puckered his wizened lips and tapped a finger against an emaciated cheek.

Tears were streaming Daimon's own cheeks and clearing his vision: *if each and every worldling carried within them the mechanics of the machine and the mechanics of magic, even…*

'Darling?' The edge in Maling's voice sharpened.

…then might they not also carry the mechanics of happiness?

'You'll never want for anything. And you'll never be unhappy again.' Maling's voice teetered towards desperation.

And conviction rose like heat through Daimon; there was still a way he could make Yann proud of him. He heard himself saying, 'I don't believe…'

Maling's face froze, in a mortified expression.

'…in you or in your machine.'

The light beams supporting Maling began flickering.

'Happiness to all worldlings!' declared Daimon.

And the illusion was broken—Maling screaming, shrivelling, his last juices draining.

The machine imploding, destroying Daimon.

But the magic, which had been so selfishly stolen, was returned to the world in a fine crystal rain.

And it all began again.

18

Submission

Thursday morning you open your laptop to find a 'throwback' that's already raised a few wry comments. There you are, as you were then—Hoxton fin, pierced everything, doing a knock-off Bowie and Ronson. And fellating guitar strings.

What the fuck were you thinking?

Back then, you were thinking how the lights would dim. How the audience would scream. How dry ice would pump in as the band took their positions. On drums, Gary. On bass, Andy. On guitar, Danny—in head to toe PVC. And at centre, yours truly—in silhouette and sheerest black, you would pause for dramatic effect before assaulting the microphone with your opening song.

Submission. Going down, down, dragging me down.

And as it ended in a sweet symphony of distortion, a million mouths would begin whooping as you went down on Danny's instrument.

Submission. I can't tell you what I've found.

You'd found the fiction broken by a bored monotone.

'Simon...'

The dry ice had dispersed, along with the imagined audience, and just one person was stood alone under the hall's harsh lighting—rolling her eyes in your direction.

'Hi Mum.'

She'd come to tell you to pack-up rehearsing—the building was closing. She must have taken the picture on her phone before interrupting. No, hang on. It was 2001. Camera phones hadn't been invented yet. She must have taken a Snappy Snap and—twenty years on—scanned it in for the world to remark upon.

Thanks, Mum.

Your mother has always liked to make a stir. Outside the hall, some minutes later, you remember her swooshing a Westwood scarf over shoulder before grabbing Danny by the ear.

'I do hope you're not sparking up on school premises, young man?'

'Sorry, Ms Thorne.'

Danny cowered in the playground like he was twelve again.

'Karen! Miss Thorne makes me feel fucking ancient.'

'Fucking *are* ancient,' you'd sneered.

Mum had let go Danny's lobe to lock the hall, and now she reached for the joint, as if to prove a point. No, wait—that can't have happened. She must have been deputy head by then!

'Sounded great tonight.' She took a drag—you're sure of it. 'Reminded me of my first Pistols gig in '76.'

'Sick!'

Danny grabbed the joint back.

'Danny, I have to say—I found your playing particularly sexy.'

What can you say? Mum has never had much by way of boundaries.

'Thank you, Ms… Karen.'

Danny was Danny, lanky and spotty.

'You need a lift home?'

She couldn't possibly have found him or his playing sexy.

'No thanks, Mum.' You took Danny's arm. 'We've got other plans.'

'You're so lucky,' Danny mused, passing the joint to you.

'Yeah.'

Truth was, you wished she'd be like your mother not your sister.

Then Danny threw a non sequitur: 'We are all in the gutter...'

You were actually in the cemetery, staring at a sequin sky. Everyone assumed the two of you were boyfriends but you were just best-friends, had been since year seven. You would've been doing A-Levels by then, Wilde quotation your new favourite thing. And while you were 'looking at the stars', it had happened for the first time: for one split second there were *two* Simons. The usual you was still sat smoking. But a different you was standing, looking down on him.

'Do you ever wonder,' you heard yourself saying, 'if there's something out there...'

And then the two separate Simons joined back together as you joined white dots in the sky with the joint's red embers.

'...something to complete the picture?'

Danny pondered for all of two seconds.

'Nah.'

You liked sixth-form: no uniform and a television in the common room. But lunchtime the day after that rehearsal, and not far into autumn term, regular programming was brought down by a bulletin. You all stared in shocked fascination as the images kept repeating. Plane crashing. Tower burning. Plane crashing, tower burning. Tower falling, tower falling. And—you can see it now—they were already building a wall from the rubble. A wall which split the world in two. They said you have to choose: are you one of us or one of them? And Danny called across the room, 'Karim, aren't you a Muslim?'

Karim was someone you had never spoken to. You'd never needed to: everyone knew he was the most boring boy in school. Didn't drink, didn't smoke. But he was pretty cute. And you've always had a soft spot for a bearded brunette.

It must've been a few weeks on—when the world was *crescendo*ing towards confrontation, and everyone was signing *pianissimo* peace petitions—that he was asked to do a presentation to sixth-form. Ms Thorne-slash-Karen-slash-Mum gave a gushing introduction.

'Experience of other cultures is *so* important. Especially at the moment.'

You leant an ear, grudgingly. He was nervous, obviously, and began inauspiciously.

'We can do what we want to do, they say. Be who we want to be...'

'I bet his cock's tiny,' Danny whispered in your ear.

Mum-slash-Karen glared at the pair of you over her designer eyewear.

'We can be popstars or politicians,' Karim went on, 'footballers or financial consultants. We can be straight or gay... but are we happy?'

Danny was so happy, so gay, that he'd begun laughing. You didn't join in: Karim had got your attention.

'The statistics don't say that we are—five hundred and twenty-five boys under the age of twenty-four took their own lives last year.'

You didn't need to look at Mum to see her tensing; you'd promised to never try *that* again.

'Happiness cannot come from complete freedom. Happiness can only come from submission. And that's the meaning of Islam.'

That was the second time it happened, the splitting. But that time it wasn't like an out-of-body experience. It was like your head was a room. And in that room were two Simons. And each of your eyes was a window that one of the Simons was staring through. As Karim looked up from his notes and caught you staring, was he seeing the old you or the new one?

'If anyone would like to learn more, please come find me in the common room.'

'Your Mum make that?'

Karim looked up from his lunchbox—lovingly-packed with portioned fruits and phallic wraps. Seeing you approach, he tensed for a fight.

You made a peace-offering. 'Crisp?' And instantly regretted it—you knew almost nothing about Muslims, but were pretty certain they didn't eat bacon.

He shook his head and offered, 'Cola?'

It was made by *Mecca*. And wasn't bad, you seem to remember.

'Not touching anything American, at the moment.'

Operation Enduring Freedom—and what a feat of endurance that turned out to be, in the end—was just then kicking off in Afghanistan. Danny was kicking off across the common-room. Probably someone had made the schoolboy error of gay-baiting him and—wit always sharpened—he was now slaying them. You got up to join the fun, leaving Karim alone again. With an invitation to join you on the protest that weekend.

It'd been twice the turnout anyone had been expecting. *Stop the War Coalition. British Association of Muslims.* Placards blending to the horizon.

Your mum had mixed feelings. *I don't support the bombing. But I do think we need to send a clear message to them.* So she went shopping.

Karim's mum came—headscarfed and hesitant, her first

demonstration. She'd packed lunch for everyone, as delicious as her son—about whom you had mixed feelings.

'So, what's it like to be a Muslim?' you said, to start the conversation.

'What's it like to be a Christian?' he said, shrugging, as the march shuffled into motion.

'Don't know. Never been one.'

Mum has always been a paid-up member of multiculturalism. But the only *Religion* she can countenance is the clothing brand. Karim had made an effort with *his* clothing—trainers and tee matching, between them surprisingly on-trend denim.

'Being Muslim is just part of who I am.'

His eyes were grey-green and just stunning. Again, you weren't sure at which Simon he was looking. The new Simon checked that Karim's mum wasn't listening.

'What, like being gay is part of who I am?'

The old Simon couldn't give a shit if she found that shocking.

Karim stared at slow-moving pavement. 'So, what is it you want to know then?'

'Um…' Good question. 'You said something about happiness coming from submission?'

Clearly this was ground he felt more comfortable on:

'I suppose I was saying that when we can do anything, *be* anything, when we've got all this *enduring freedom*, we can find ourselves despairing at the lack of direction, and Islam…'

For the new you, this was resonating. Like somewhere deep inside, almost out of hearing, a bass string was thrumming.

'A Muslim submits to Allah, yeah? And submitting to something bigger than us, something we can all be part of… brings happiness.'

'Karim.' His Mum was *definitely* listening by then. 'Why not bring him to mosque if he wants to know Islam?'

So you hadn't scared her off with your piercings.

'Mama, no...'

'Thank you,' sang the *New You*. 'I'd like to.'

You met Karim at the school gates on Friday afternoon: he was grudging, and in your gut, Old You was groaning. By the time you reached the mosque, Old You was wailing so loud in there you were sure everyone could hear. Karim explained, 'That's the call to prayer.'

And many had answered... African, Asian, European. You joined them. Caps, headscarves. All shades, all patterns. The mosque an orange brick building with blue brick patterning. Beside it, two blue-clad policemen.

'They've been here since the bombings.' Yasmine was more welcoming than her son. 'Shall we go in?'

You were following her when Karim pulled you in the other direction. 'That way's for women.' There was no third way for transgendered and non-binary.

Boots had to be left outside. Yours had eight-eyelets. Nightmare to get off.

'I have to wash.'

And so Karim left you looking at a hole in your sock, as the men around you stared—even though you'd flattened your hair—and Old You screamed *run*.

If Karim hadn't come back just then, you might well have done.

The prayer hall was all white-wall minimal. Mum would have approved. Not of the carpet though. She would have thought that shrill. But it did have a good pile. Some guys greeted

Karim with words you did not understand. He didn't introduce you and Yasmine was nowhere to be seen.

'There's another hall for women,' Karim filled you in.

The men's hall was filling. A guy with his back to everyone started singing. The other guys formed lines behind him. Karim said you should sit up back. He joined the kneeling men. Who then started chanting. More words you couldn't understand. You were feeling stupid, all at sea. Suddenly, a wave of rears rose in the air as they pressed foreheads to the floor.

What the fuck?

You knew you couldn't contain it much longer.

What the fuck are you doing here?

Soon Old You would burst into anger, or laughter. And you'd like to extend your apologies, retrospectively, to that man who turned to glare: you didn't mean to disrespect anyone's religion. You were only eighteen. You didn't know what you wanted, back then.

'So where did you disappear to?'

The Monday after. You slammed your locker, sealing the Placebo poster inside its door. Karim was stood there.

'I, uh…' What happened was, you'd slipped out before anyone else heard you laughing. 'I'm sorry.'

He eyed you coolly, green-grey. It was your turn to look away. 'Mum said I should give you this.'

When you looked up again there was a book in his hand.

'Alright Si?' Danny sauntered by with one of his ironic glances. Your cool evaporated instantly. 'Alright K'rimie?'

Karim ignored him. 'It's the Quran.'

Hardbacked, it hung heavy between you. Over Karim's shoulder, you could see Danny wiggling a little finger. There was little doubt what he meant to imply. And you doubted he could be jealous: you and Danny were like brothers.

Karim brought you back to the matter in hand: 'You don't have to take it.'

Was he offering a way out? Or perhaps, wanting one?

'Thanks.'

With Danny watching, New You took the Quran.

That night, New You was reading—it was back to front and bloody hard-going—while Old You was sulking.

Can't we turn the light out?

Not yet.

Then can't we have a wank instead?

The door opened. 'Simon, you taken your pills this evening?'

'Yes, Mum!'

She scrunched her eyes small, said, 'What are you hiding?'

You pulled the covers tighter, said nothing.

'Is it porn?'

See? No boundaries.

'Show me!'

She ignored all denials and, unable to lever your double-locked fingers, went in for the tickle.

'Honestly, I can't believe you've got dick pics under there and you're not going to share!'

'Fuck off!'

'Fuck off yourself.'

'I need some space!'

She retreated then. 'Space, Simon, is something I've never stopped you having.'

'That's just your trouble. You're too fucking liberal.'

'Too… liberal?'

'Yes!'

Twenty years on, you know how ridiculous it sounds.

'Right!' She turned on her teacher voice, smile set in rigor mortis. 'Next time you're bleeding all over the bleeding carpet this bleeding heart will just leave you to it.'

And out she swept.

You'd not got anywhere with the reading, not really, so a few days later you popped into the local library. No internet on your phone back then. You're not sure you even had it at home. Of course, it was in school. But you wanted to be somewhere no one knew you. New You wanted to believe Islam *cool*; Old You was certain no one else would think so.

Leaning into the screen, you typed your query into the search engine.

Can you be gay and Muslim?

The first result linked to a quote from the Quran.

Do you commit the worst sin such as none preceding you has committed in mankind or jinn? Old You thought gin was something Mum necked with tonic. *Verily you practise your lusts on men instead of women.*

The second led to *Al-Fatiha Foundation* for LGBT Muslims. New You saw an opening.

'Hello there,' someone said quietly in your ear.

You jumped so loudly everyone could probably hear, quickly made the search window disappear, and turned to find Yasmine at your shoulder, wearing a brightly-patterned headscarf and a smile almost ear to ear.

'What are you doing here?' you asked her.

'I work here.' Had she seen something? 'What are you doing?'

'Just, um...' Someone was tutting over your whispered conversation. '...Going.'

And so was Yasmine. Home to make Karim's tea.

'Does your Mum cook for you?' she asked as you walked together up Ladbroke Grove.

'She makes sure the fridge is always full.'

'I expect she's very busy at school.'

You stopped on the corner of Oxford Gardens. 'Bye, then.'

You knew she lived in one of the blocks behind Golborne.

'You know, Karim never has friends home.' She was frowning but smiling. 'If you wanted to come for food, you'd be welcome.'

'Is it hard to be a Muslim?'

'You mean, at the moment, with this *hate crime* they're reporting?'

'I mean, are there lots of rules and regulations?'

'I think certain men make much of them. Without faith, they mean nothing.'

You took the lift with her to the top floor. 'So how do you become a Muslim, then?'

'You make a declaration.' She ushered you through the door—inside, it smelt of soup and soap powder. 'Karim, look who's here!'

His bedroom was as neat as his person—instead of the usual pinned posters of popstars, there were framed scripts, presumably Arabic. The view was pretty neat too—like a monochrome painting, with broad strokes of council concrete and fine lines of Victorian terracing.

'That's my house, look!'

Once he was over the surprise of seeing you there, Karim

was more relaxed than you'd seen him before—like he wasn't worried who was watching him here.

'Where?' He leaned in to see better.

'On the corner.' Your shoulder touched his shoulder.

'Oh yeah.' He seemed happy with the physical proximity.

You felt higher than you ever had smoking weed. 'From up here, all the streetlights and stars look like you could join them together and a picture would appear.'

'Of what?' His eyes, reflecting in the pane, seemed brighter than any star.

'Not sure. Allah?'

The pane misted with his laughter. 'There are no images of Allah.'

'Why not?'

He looked at you direct. 'Google it.'

And you wanted to tell him you had been googling. You wanted to tell him you'd been thinking. Of everything he'd been saying. Of nothing but him.

'You know what you said about submission…' And you were so mixed-up then, you weren't certain which of You—Old or New—was talking, but you heard yourself saying, 'I think I might want to be Muslim.'

'You're sure?' Karim double-checked as you re-entered the mosque, some weeks later.

You weren't sure, but New You nodded at him, wrestling Old You into submission: curd and whey had separated conclusively by that time. And by the time Karim had led you to the Imam's door, you'd gathered a trail like the Pied Piper. Not of mice but men, and once within, they offered their hands. You shook them. They told you their names. You forgot them. They asked what had prompted your interest in Islam.

Penile circumcision? Old You sat snarking.

New You rubbed your head, de-mohawked for the occasion. 'I've been unhappy for a long time—with myself, with the materialist world we're living in…'

Heads around you were nodding.

'So much so, I…' You'd never even told this to Karim. '…I tried to kill myself a few years ago.'

Around you, heads were shaking.

'Mum thinks it's depression. That it can all be cured with medication. But I know it's not about serotonin. I feel like something's missing.'

You looked at Karim; he was frowning and smiling.

'And then I met Karim and…' You'd spent evening after evening in his room studying the Quran. And the lines in his forehead. His cheeks, dimpling. 'I think that the missing something is Islam.'

Karim was extended a congratulatory murmur. And you were told how pleased they were to have you there. How Muslims were not terrorists or extremists. How Islam was kind and moderate.

'You cannot pull lines from the Quran at random,' said the Imam. 'It must be read as a whole—it is direct revelation.'

He extended a hand.

'Now, will you make your declaration?'

You'd knelt on the carpet, repeating after him until you got it right. 'La ilaha allallahu wa Muhammadur rasulullah. La ilaha allallahu wa Muhammadur rasulullah. There is no God but Allah and Muhammad is his messenger.' You'd been handed from man to man, blown with best wishes from their palms, limbs light as dandelion.

Then gravity had kicked in.

'How you feeling?'

Karim had come home with you for the first time—a calm in the chaos of your room.

'I don't feel any different.'

You'd been trying to get shit in order, pulling down posters. *Placebo—how apt*, Old You snapped; you pushed him back into his corner.

Karim took your arm. 'You only just made your declaration.'

'When are you making yours then?'

And with a force equal and opposite—like that law you'd learnt in physics—Old You bounced back into the ring and was kissing Karim, your blossoming beards brushing.

Karim pulled away. 'I can't.'

'Why?'

'It's the *worst sin*.'

'You can't pull lines at random from the Quran. I have it on authority from the Imam.'

You kissed him a second time. He stopped resisting.

'Simon?'

Mum interrupted with a slam of the front door. Karim retreated as her footsteps slammed upstairs. By then, she knew better than to enter without knocking. You told her to come in.

'Are those bags outside yours…?' She stopped, dead, in the door. 'Oh my god! What have you done to your hair?'

'I've gone Sinéad O'Connor.'

'Karim!' She spotted your guest, in the corner. 'I wasn't expecting to see you here.' She looked from one buzzed head to the other, at the wisps of chin hair, and couldn't get the pieces to jigsaw. 'When I said hands off my razors, I didn't mean stop shaving altogether... So, what's with the bin liners?'

'Just some stuff I don't need any more.'

She noticed the walls were bare. 'Well, don't leave them lying outside the front door—you know where the dustbins are.' And she gave you that look which said *we'll talk about this later*. 'Karim, you want dinner? There's pizza in the freezer.'

'No, thank you, Ms Thorne.'

'*Karen*. I'll leave you boys to it, then.'

With a fling of her cost-a-bomb hair, she was gone.

Karim was frowning. 'When are you going to tell her?'

'When are you telling yours?'

Mum's place was Habitat immaculate; the cleaner saw to that. Yasmine's was cluttered and colourful; the seats were actually comfortable. You were sat around the table and the remains of another delicious meal.

'You think I did not know?' Yasmine's head was shaking. 'Men have always done these things. Your own father...' Her husband had been older, had died when Karim was young. 'Peace be upon him.' To spare her son's squirming, she did not go on.

'Of course, there are also men—some of them are our family and friends—who will not admit such things happen, will not admit such things are even possible in Islam.' Her frown gave way to smiling. 'We will have to be clever with them, but when we are home...'

She unpinned her hijab to reveal hair that was natural, beautiful.

'Simon, you are family, now.'

Monday morning—high on contradiction and deep in conversation with your new boyfriend—you didn't see Danny approaching.

'What happened to you, then?'

Shit. Gary's eighteenth. With everything going on you'd clean forgotten.

'How was it?' you winced.

'Got so wasted I snogged Andy's brother.'

'Yeah?'

If Danny was trying to make you jealous, it wasn't working. You looked over at Karim, pretending to be looking for something in his locker.

'I'm not really drinking anymore.'

Danny's eyes widened. 'After the first glass…' Another Wilde quotation. 'You don't know what you're missing out on.' His eyes narrowed in Karim's direction. 'I hope you've not forgotten the gig Friday evening?'

You assured him you hadn't.

When two *yous* interact, it is with actions equal and opposite. What followed may seem like the coup of the New. But the Old got off on the shock of it all.

School hall full. This time, for real.

As lights dimmed and dry ice sputtered in, the band took their positions.

On drums, Gary.

On bass, Andy.

On guitar, Danny—dressed casually.

At centre, yours falsely—in silhouette and floor-length black, you paused to no effect, before torturing the microphone with your opening song.

'Submission. Down, down, *life was* dragging me down.'

And as it was ending, you went down to a kneeling position.

'Submission. I *can* tell you *that* I've found...'

The band stopped distorting, thrown by this deviation.

'La ilaha allallahu wa Muhammadur rasulullah. La ilaha al-lallahu wa Muhammadur rasulullah. There is no God but Allah and Muhammad is his messenger.'

In the crowd's silence, you could hear *her* voice dropping.

'Simon?'

What the fuck did you think would happen?

That the audience would join this public declaration, made a week on from that private one in the Imam's room? Wrong. They started laughing, booing, throwing coke cans. And still you didn't feel any different.

That a seven-year friendship would survive such public humiliation? Wrong. Danny swept from stage, never to have 'bon mot' for you again. *Each man kills the thing he loves,* and all that. If you could tag him in Mum's pic—*remember this*—you might find out if he's forgiven you yet.

That your boyfriend would be overcome with emotion by your public pageant? Karim certainly looked like he'd been crying. He was outside the school gates, waiting. You still had on your make-up and the *thobe* you'd been given by his Mum.

'Congratulations. That was my religion you were mocking.'

'I wasn't...'

'It's all an act with you, isn't it? Look at me, Mum, aren't I shocking—I'm a Muslim.'

Wrong.

Karim went back to sitting alone in the common room. And Yasmine never tapped your shoulder in the library again.

But there was one thing you were right on.

'How very Cat Stevens, yawn.' Mum marched into your room without knocking, blood finally drawn. 'So, tell me, do they cut off the hand or the cock these days?'

'What?'

'SIMON! YOU'RE *GAY*!'

'And?'

'You know, I'm really not buying the whole *liberal Islam* thing. All those academics in headscarves feeling *free from the male gaze*. Bollocks! They're wearing them because men want them to wear them. It's good old-fashioned repression. Took a lot of blood, sweat and years to get something even vaguely approaching equality. For you and for me! And I don't intend to stand by and see you throw it away!'

'Well, fuck off then!'

She slapped you around the face then for the first—and last—time.

'I think you'll find a Muslim respects their parents!'

She didn't *stand by*, but she did stand by *you*. All of you. All the Simons you tried to become—Muslim, vegan, BDSM. And now you have a 'boy' of your own, you see that—sometimes— we all just need a firm hand.

Beneath Mum's post, you add a wry comment of your own. And an eye-roll emoticon.

19

Only Connect

Hi

                                      Hello.

Cool profile

                                      Thanks.

How's u?

                                  Good. You?

I'm good top
*too

                                       Ha!

Love ur tattoos

                              None yourself?

Not yet
Wanna get some though

                          Then you should do.

And piercings

                   I see you have your ears done.

Yeah
Wanna stretch them

                                    Nice.

Yr dick pierced?

                                Of course,

Fuck!

Never been with a guy with a piercing

> You've not lived.

Wld luv to try

> Maybe I could help you with that.

How long you had it?

> Since I was about your age.

How old u now?

> As it says on the profile. And you?

Nearly 20

> A 21st Century Boy.

Ahaha yeah

> So what would you want piercing?

Septum

> Well I am rather partial to a young man
> with a septum ring.

Lol

> I might even be tempted
> to do it myself.

U a piercer?

> I've pierced some boys before.

Would b up for that

> Hot.

;)

Stretch it big.

Make you a proper little pig.

Oink

Do those ears while we're at it.

Big as yrs?

At least.

Please

Where else wld u wanna pierce me?

Nipples. Definitely.

That make them more sensitive?

Oh yes. Especially when
the rings are nice and heavy.

Mm yeah

Modified for Sir's pleasure

Good Boy. Very.

:)

I now have a semi.

Me too

We'll get a ring through that as well.

Fuck yes!

Sir may mod me as he wishes

Make me his perfect boy

Thank you, Boy.

What else wd Sir like to do to me?

I see you've been
letting yourself get hairy.

Sorry Sir

I like my boys smooth.

Ok sir

I suppose I'll have to sort it for you.

I think you will

Might just make your ass smooth too.

Yes SIR!

Does Sir want me smooth all over?

Ever had your
head shaved by a Sir?

Never

I love to see a boy's hair fall to the floor.

Horny as

I love shaving a boy until he shines.
Making him mine.

Can't wait for Sir to get out his razor
Sir and Boi can b skinheads together

Completely
smoothed for my pleasure.

Completely owned boy
Exactly how I wannabe

Exactly how you ARE, Boy.

Keep me that way
I have no say

Your hair is yours no longer.

Show me who's boss
Show me my place as ur sub

Gonna shave you beautiful.

Eyebrows?

Eyebrows is weird.
Those you can keep. And your beard.

Tatts too?

Yes, let's get you tattooed.

My appearance controlled

What/where would they be?

Sir can decide for me
Somewhere public
Masters marked object
Or somewhere humiliating
?

Humiliation isn't my thing.

K

Sorry.

It's fine
Doesn't have to b humiliating

Why would you want to be

humiliated anyway?

Dunno

Just a fetish

Never thought about it

Right.

Why'd u wanna shave my head?

Fair point.

But humiliation is different.

If u say so

Were you never bullied at school?

Not really

Nothing bad anyway

Maybe times HAVE changed.

Yeah

Maybe.

Still there?

Sir?

I was in the changing room at the swimming pool, recently. There was a group of boys in. They were about ten or eleven, I would say. Then one of them asks me, 'Are you gay?'

Ok...

It's a long time since I hid it from anyone, so I tell him I am. And before you know it,

they're all shouting, 'He's a rapist.
Don't go near him.'

Wow

At first, I try to reason. Educate them.
'Do you even know what that means?'

Prob not

That just makes matters worse, of course.
They start taking the piss out of my voice.

Little shits

So then I ignore them. Get dressed
as quickly as I can. But inside
I'm ten and back in the playground,
being humiliated all over again.

: (

And by the time I'm leaving, the boldest
of them—the one who asked the question—
is squaring up to me in the doorway, asking
again and again, 'Are you really gay?'
Like he can't believe I would admit
to a thing of which I should be so ashamed.
And I want to hit him. But I can't. He's ten.
By the time I get to reception to say
something to the woman I burst out
crying. I'm forty-one.

79

I'm sorry that happened

                              So that's why
                        I can't do humiliation.

I wld've give em a good kick

                          They were just kids.
                Their parents, on the other hand…

I think u gotta own it?

                                Own what?

Like yeah I'm a faggot
And I love it
All that shit you wanna hurt me with?
I get off on it

                          So it's cathartic?

What's that?

                 Releasing repressed emotions
                      in order to relieve them.

Ok

                        Like in the theatre.

You an actor?

                     I've trodden some boards.

So fetish is like playing a part I guess
U become someone else
Something else

                              Okay.

I suppose they're both a sort of 'play'.

U know you watch porn
and the acting sometimes
It's so bad it's funny
U got to get into it

Suspend your disbelief?

Same with fetish
You give control to someone else
Everything's more intense
Pain pleasure
Like u got no borders
Like ur part of the same thing
Part of each other

You should write poetry.

Maybe
Fetish is just fantasy
I mean you really gonna pierce me?

Possibly.

(still could btw)

Good to know, Boy.

;-)

You see, I understand transformation:
that's about enhancing, not degrading.

Stop thinking

81

so much bout everything
Meant to be fun

> You know, Boy, I think we have things
> we could teach each other.

:-)

> Fancy a drink?

Sure
Sir
Where?

> In a bar?

Alright

> Meet. Chat. Connect.

When?

> Carpe diem.

?

> Seize the day.
> Or night, in this case.
> It's Latin.

Sir is a fountain of wisdom

> Cheeky fucker.

;-p

> So what are you doing later?

Meeting you Sir

> Good Boy. Great.

You know, you're very cute.

Thx

Sir is v handsome

By the way, what's your name?

20

Going Up, Going Down

It's Mother's seventieth, so I'm home for the weekend armed with orchids (her favourite). She made it quite clear to *everybody* that she didn't want a party, or any surprises. The surprise was mine when I walked in to find she's treated herself to a new three-piece recliner in red pleather, quite out of proportion to the sitting room (and quite of character with its Anaglypta wallpaper).

Fish pie for dinner, and now we're all feet in the air—toes almost touching across the coffee table, and our *digestifs* in danger of being kicked from their coasters—me and the husband on the sofa, Mother and Father in their armchairs. There's a rerun of some old-school drama on the television—all heaving bosoms and mouths full of plums—when—*oh my god*, it's him! Doe-eyed and drippy-fringed, just as I first remember him.

But then my memory (like much of me) is not what it used to be. I can just see the clock, cross-haired at the end of Beaumont Street, and me in the backseat, ready to shoot or be shot. Though really, it can't have been like that: Beaumont must have been double yellow-lined even then, and the car parked in some side-street—the three of us waiting, necks craning, for those gilded hands to minute towards eleven.

Dad has always been a devotee of contingency so of course we were early—the three of us steaming the windscreen, wipers metronoming, fluffy dice swinging. Or maybe by then Mum had exchanged the dice for a similarly fluffy Forever Friend. The one she'd given me was mortar-boarded; this meant they

87

were proud: first in the family to go to university and I *only went and got into Oxford,* didn't I?

'Prawn cocktail…' Mum was distributing snacks from a knapsack on her lap. 'Graham won't want them.'

She wasn't wrong: flesh had not passed my lips since I'd heard Morrissey declare *Meat Is Murder* some years earlier.

'Cheese and Onion?'

It can't have been The Smiths playing, I'm certain, as Dad would've been listening to their archenemy, Radio One. But music of some kind, and Mum's interruptions were ruining my concentration: I was reading. Possibly the Complete-Shakespearean tome I'd won in school prize giving.

Hamlet was my favourite: *Ay, madam, it is common.*

As, I thought, were crisps. 'No thanks, Mum.'

'Someone just got out that car!' Dad drew our attention to a motor rather newer than our own but similarly piled with possessions, and to a guy running through the rain.

I didn't know it then, but it was him.

'He's going in!'

'Go on, Graham!'

'It's not time!'

Mother's perm shook. Was it still permed by that point? Probably not: we'd left the eighties behind a few years back and hair had straightened out. 'Well, if you're not going, I am!'

The thought of her talking for me—of her saying the wrong thing—was enough to send me running.

Approaching those college portals, I was Dorothy approaching The Emerald City. There was no knocker, just a buzzer. But a door incised inside the main one did swing open. The guy from the other car was there—handsome as a young Hugh Grant in

Maurice (which, to Mum's disgust, I'd stayed up to watch). His voice was so loud, so clear it might have rung the bell above us in the clock tower.

'After you.'

'Thank you.'

My voice came without its own amplification system. I stepped in, the door clicked shut, and he was gone.

Freshers coming up please report to the Porter's Lodge, instructed the sign. Which—where I'd come from—translated as *new arrivals report to reception.*

The porter had a funny uniform, though not in emerald green; I summoned my most confident articulation and gave my name, scanning the grander-sounding ones on the pigeonholes surrounding us as he dived down his list, almost to the bottom.

'Waterman. Staircase seven. Room nine.'

The door opened and—key in one hand, the other balancing a box brimming with mugs, cutlery and some 'fancy teas' Mum had got on offer in Sainsbury's—I stepped in. Magnolia and modern, the room was a disappointment. Hoping to avoid loans and get by on my grant alone, I'd taken the cheapest option. But still, I'd been envisaging something more… grandiloquent.

'I'd have nets up those windows.' Mother had materialised at my shoulder and was looking down her nose at the *quadrangle* below.

'It's my room, and I'll do what I want with it.'

I'd overstepped: she dropped the case she'd carried up, just missing my feet.

'Best get the rest before it gets wet.'

At the gate, Dad gave me a hug. 'Do us proud,' he muttered, before ducking into the driver's seat as quick as he could.

Was it the rain making Mum's mascara run? Her hug lasted long enough for me to clock the guy again—fringe dripping, eyes blinking, waving off his parents in their Volkswagen.

'Come on, Susan!'

Dad's always been reluctant to take up space someone else could be taking, and outside the gate, cars were beeping. I told Mother I'd *call soon* and then they were gone.

I could be my own person.

Something maudlin from Morrissey's latest album was probably playing, and in the background, the walls would've been freshly-plastered with his image as I looked my own over in the mirror. A shiny suit (fifty quid in Dewsbury market) jarred with headstrong hair (alas, no longer). I attempted to *cap* it and checked my invite.

'Shite.' Unlike my father, I'm always late.

I was adjusting my *gown* when Professor Gordon's heavy wooden door swung open. 'Ah, Master Waterman. We were wondering when you were going to join.'

He'd already been *joined* by two other students—chatting under oak beams, caps under arm. The *guy* was one of them. I felt myself blushing—for not knowing the correct clothing etiquette. I brushed off my mortarboard, took the hands I was offered. Charlotte and, of course, Guy. Unlike mine, their palms were dry.

The professor handed me a sherry. 'Are you settling in okay?'

'Yes, thank you.' I sipped politely.

'Where are you from?' asked Lottie (as she preferred to be known).

'West Yorkshire.' I found her interest unnerving.

'I was trying to work out the accent.' Her pronunciation was the received one.

Guy's too: 'Which school?'

'Just a comprehensive… And you?'

Guy had been to Eton, Lottie to Bryanston. She'd been travelling since leaving.

'India was life-changing.'

I'd spent my gap year working and saving.

'With my dad,' I explained. 'He's a… contractor.'

Guy had also interned with his father—but at the Duke of York theatre.

As we toddled to the *refectory* (aka the dining room), I realised I shouldn't have had that second sherry. By the time starters started arriving, I was starving. Back home, dinner was at dinnertime. And tea was six not seven. No idea which silverware I should be using, I copied Lottie.

'I can't believe your father is Teddy Terry!'

Since discovering Guy's dad was one of those actors who popped up periodically in period dramas, she'd lost all interest in me and was talking over my head to Guy—who'd been seated on my other side. Either side of them sat *subfusc*ed students (suited and gowned) at tables which forked, three-tined, to a *high table* of *dons* whose framed-forbears hung over them.

White-gloved waiters worked the room with wine; my pores were pouring: Mum always said *red with meat and white with fish* but what about vegetarian? White was what we'd had at home. Christmas and special occasions. But the wine I sat sipping was nothing like *Blue Nun*. I wasn't sure I liked it. Or the beer, later in the bar.

The more I drank, the harder it became to keep my desire *curtained* each time Guy's eyes came in my direction. But they weren't really coming for me—why would they? Anyone could see his eyes were only for Lottie, whose interest was—by that point—quite naked. Everyone around us was so bright, so brilliant, that I didn't feel I could join the conversation. Knowing no-one would miss me, I took a last sip and out I slipped—from old quad to new, new room, new bed—lyrics already forming in my head.

And if you're so clever, why do you sleep alone tonight?

Morrissey. Before he unbuttoned that sequined skin and a belligerent old badger stepped from within.

Love is natural and real, but not for such as you and I, my love.

CD spinning, I lay listening.

Oh mother, I can feel the soil falling over my head.

Cuddling the teddy Mum had given me like the best Brideshead cliché.

When I woke in the morning, it took a moment to ascertain that the pounding was not in my cranium, but on the door to my room. Hearing it open, I retrieved some semblance of clothing from the floor and—rounding the corner from my sleeping area—found a woman stood there.

'Just emptying the bin.' She must have been about the same age as Mum; she was wearing a uniform. 'I'm Brenda.' And was that a Yorkshire accent? 'Your scout.'

Scout was what they called their cleaners.

'Graham,' was all I could muster.

'Don't worry, I won't be touching your CDs or anything.' Bypassing the music system I'd been given when I got through the entrance exam, she seamlessly lifted liner from bin and lowered in a fresh one. 'My son goes berserk if I get near his.'

And then she was gone, her fleeting familiarity leaving an unexpected pang. The digits of the music system told me it was after ten: Mum would be heading home from her own cleaning round.

The phone was at the bottom of the *staircase*; it must have been shared by about twenty students.

'Hello?'

I fed in a first coin.

'Hi Mum.'

An umbilical string stretched taut between her cup and mine: we were connected again.

'What you doing calling this time? Cost an arm and leg, it will!'

She wasn't wrong—the phone was eating through change—but I could tell she was made up to hear so soon from her son. As someone who had so fiercely cultivated my independence, it would've been a climb-down to admit I was missing my mum, so we talked about what I'd eaten, had I made any friends…?

'Got to go. Someone's waiting.'

Indeed, I could see feet tapping on the first landing—but she's always known how to read me, even when I think I'm giving nothing away.

'You'll meet people soon, Graham.'

Certain Mother hadn't meant *this*, I hurried to Brasenose College, fingering the flyer in my pocket.

Too nervous to visit us at Fresher's Fair? Come here.

Xeroxed and blanket *pigeon-posted*, the anonymous missive may as well have been addressed directly, because my nerves had indeed got the better of me.

I'd signed for the *Union*—pricey, but the first few debates were free—and *Oxford University Dramatic Society*. I was debating whether I dared enter *Cuppers*—their competition for freshers—when I found myself rabbited in the headlamps of a *Gaysoc* stallholder—for what seemed hours—before hop-skipping to the safety of the *Music Society.*

Now I skipped again, past the *Russell Room.* Even if I hadn't learnt the name by heart—terrified I might have to pull that pink paper from my pocket—I would've known I was in the right place, signposted as it was from the Lodge, bold as bollocks. I loitered under cloisters, sublimating fear into Shakespeare—*now might I do it pat*—while attempting to look casual. Casual was the look I'd gone for that evening—nothing too gay—Morrissey *Your Arsenal* tee, blackest jeans, DMs (obligatory). No-one was going in, so I sauntered back past, trying to *see* in. But the shutters were down. Then two guys breezed by and—casual as anything—bowled straight in. Without allowing myself another *muddy-mettled* moment, I followed them.

In a room far from full, the air was full-fruited with sibilance. Mother's voice rose above them, saying *people like us aren't like that.* I should never have come, and hid behind hair-curtains as I bee-lined for the bar.

'Didn't expect to see you here.'

I was draining my plastic chalice when Guy entered stage left, handsome.

'I could say the same.'

I felt myself turning the colour of my wine—I'd tried red that evening.

'Graham—Julian.'

Guy had a gentleman with him.

'Charmed.'

The gentleman offered a flaccid hand.

'Another?' Guy offered. And as he headed for the bar, my eyes followed him like he were a lifeboat off Newfoundland.

'Can't say I think much of the talent.' Julian was surveying the scene. 'So how do you know Guy then?' His eyebrow arched for the ceiling.

'Uh… Um…' Battling as I was with basic phonetics, who would have guessed I'd come *up* to Oxford to study English? 'He's in my tutor group… How do you know him?'

'Intimately,' Julian moued, maleficently.

Guy sailed back over, my rubber-ring bearer.

'So how long have you been out, then?'

'I'm not.' I gulped more wine. 'My parents wouldn't understand.'

'I thought that. But mine were fine.'

'Darling, please!' Julian slapped Guy on the shoulder, playfully. 'Teddy Terry is even camper than me!'

I looked away, visions of towering phalluses conjured by even this tiny intimacy.

'It's funny: I thought you and Lottie…' I could see Guy found *that* amusing. 'She was all over you the other evening.'

'She just wants me for her Cuppers team. Pinter two-hander. You doing something?'

I steered myself between the *Scylla* of relief and *Charybdis* of jealousy.

'Maybe.'

Maybe had become *definitely* by the time I made it back to my room. But I'd barely begun battle with my Oxford *opus one* when a knock at the door forced me to down pen *and* music: probably Mozza's caterwauling was disturbing one of the neighbours whose double-barrels I was still getting to grips with. I donned my habitual self-effacement, opened the door, and found Guy's face framed there.

'I hope I'm not disturbing your studies?'

I'd left Gaysoc on the pretext of getting down to my debut essay. Indeed, that had been my intention: I was desperate to make a good first impression and couldn't comprehend the cavalier affectations of some peers. I'd worked bloody hard to get there, to get the results and—as a result—couldn't believe that I alone could be enough. This is perhaps why I've always struggled in conversation: I have to find that perfect thing to say, which almost always eludes me. And that was *really* why I'd made my excuses: I couldn't compete with sharp-tongued Julian.

The object of his affectation (and my affection) was looking even more dashing doorframed—pink college scarf matching cheeks cherubimed by an October evening.

'Do you want to come in?'

'I've not been in one of these rooms yet.' Guy lit it up.

I could barely bring myself to look at him. 'Where's yours, then?'

'Over on the old quad.' That meant one of the posh ones.

I knew you were meant to offer drinks. But alcohol—and cigarettes—weren't habits I'd pick up for some years yet: I had only Mother's selection packs.

Guy accepted Earl Grey but declined milk and sugar. This would not have been approved of by Mother. Neither would the subsequent turn in conversation.

'What happened to Julian?'

'Picked up some guy from Magdalen.'

I felt myself flushing, masked it in the kettle's steaming. 'I thought he was your boyfriend?'

'We had a fumble once in the dorm.' Guy was laughing. 'But didn't everyone?'

No. They didn't.

Look at him, looking. In school changing rooms, I'd kept my head hung. *Backs against the wall, boys.* And, oh, the horrors of communal showering.

'You must have had boyfriends?'

No. I hadn't.

If you ever turn out like that, you'll be straight out that door. Girlfriends had been taken to pacify Mother. The strap of a bra was as far as I'd ventured.

'I find that surprising.' Guy took his tea from my hand. 'I mean, you're very good-looking…'

Anyone with more self-esteem might have known what to do with that open ending; I hid behind my *Lapsang Souchong*. Socially more dextrous, Guy conjured a joke-trick from the silence: 'Are these your Wanderer wanderings?'

The Wanderer was what we were studying that term. I was struggling with its Anglo-Saxon. The language in the notebook on which Guy was advancing was a more familiar one.

'No, it's just some ideas for Cuppers.'

I moved to remove it from the desk.

'Can I look?' Without awaiting my reply, Guy started flicking. 'Is this all *your* writing?'

I nodded acquiescence: it felt like flashing.

'It's amazing.'

A little praise steamed my shell open: we talked and talked about *everything*—tea forgotten, skin forming—until Guy clocked the digits on the music system and thought it time to get back to his own room. 'Lectures in the morning.'

I could see the moment moving away from me—like Claudius rising from praying before Hamlet has decided whether (or not) to kill him.

'Or...' I stuttered when Guy was already at the door, '...you could stay here...?'

Fortunately, he knew exactly what to do with an opening.

If that first time felt momentous—and it did—it was possibly more down to a sense of occasion than any feat of sexual wizardry he may have been performing: in reality, he was probably just a bit less awkward than I was. I remember thinking *I can't believe I'm finally doing this.* I remember his cock smelling of piss. I remember falling asleep on his chest.

I woke the next morning to the sound of knocking. The door would open any second, Guy still sardined in bed beside me. I was barely twenty, the age of consent twenty-one—fear floodlit the room. And shame. Like that time when Mother walked in on me wanking.

What are you doing?

I could imagine her looking down on me in that moment, in flagrante with another man.

What have you done?

Hearing the key turning, I scrambled for clothing, calling, 'Hello?'

A voice not unlike Mother's bounced back around the corner: 'Thought you'd be in a lecture.'

Shit! Had I missed it? The first fucking lecture of term.

'I... um... not feeling great. I'm still in bed so... if you could just, you know...'

'I'll do the cleaning tomorrow.'

I could almost hear Brenda's raised eyebrow. *Did she know?* She could probably smell the testosterone.

As the door clicked shut, Guy's laughter burst behind my back. 'I'll do the cleaning tomorrow.' It was an almost perfect imitation of the scout's accent. Or mine.

I wasn't laughing. 'We missed our lecture.'

'There'll be others.'

Guy drew me back beneath the covers. And if it had been television, The Smiths' *Please, Please, Please Let Me Get What I Want* would have kicked in as a montage of *good times* began. In time, the sex would become less awkward. In time, I would come to crave the smell of him—find myself sniffing underpants he left behind one morning. I couldn't wait to be close to him each evening, spending afternoons staring from windows in the *Bodleian;* it was him and not spires of which I was dreaming. Waking tangled together, I would run fingers through his tousled hair, and Sundays we would just stay there—fucking, talking, reading the supplements. It was Guy—who knew everything, or so it seemed—who steered me from *The Times*: before him, I had no notion it was right-wing, and little that there even was such a thing; my parents read *The Sun*. And as weeks faded into each other—and on our soundtrack, mandolins soar—I grew closer and closer to him and further and further from them.

A mid-term visit. I suggested we go out for lunch but—no—they wanted to have it in hall like I did, to *get the full Oxford experience*. I wasn't as pleased to see them as I'd have expected, just a month back. And although—just over a month back—Mum had threatened to hack my *long locks off*, now that I'd done it, got the 'Hugh Grant' cut, she too didn't seem as pleased as might have been expected.

'Doesn't suit you,' she told me, a little too frankly.

I didn't think much of the C&A she was wearing, but didn't say anything.

'What does *griddled* mean?'

Dad was in his usual short-sleeve and jeans, menu on the bench before him.

'It's when they grill it in a pan.'

I rolled my eyes, conveniently forgetting I'd not long since asked Guy the same question. We'd been eating out more than I'd ever eaten out before: back home, there'd only been the odd excursion to *Harvester*.

'The salmon for me, please.'

Mother had used her posh voice to order; I averted my eyes from the waiter. I'd never really noticed her accent, but by then I couldn't bear to hear it—especially in my own mouth. Which dropped open as Guy and Lottie walked in. Guy had been instructed to steer clear; clearly that direction had not been taken by Lottie.

'Hi!'

'Mum, Dad, this is Lottie and Guy...'

'We've heard all about you,' Dad kowtowed.

Obviously, I'd been somewhat selective in what I'd told him, but hadn't shied from revealing that my new best friend was the son of someone he'd seen on his television.

'Would you like to sit down?'

That was the longest *luncheon*. To my perturbation, Guy thought it would be funny to play footsie with me while Dad asked his usual questions.

'So, what do you want to do after graduating?'

'Act.'

'And can you make a living from that?'

Guy shrugged. 'My parents have done alright.'

'His father's Teddy Terry,' Lottie reminded us, quite unnecessarily.

'I thought he was great in that thing… What was it, Susan?'

Mum—perhaps trying to read the situation—had surprisingly little to contribute to the conversation. But back in my room *she* was full of questions.

'Is Lottie Guy's girlfriend?'

I've always enjoyed a frisson, like when I pronounced the Queen *should be dead* one evening in the living room.

'He's gay, Mum.'

I could feel my temperature climbing. Dad must have gone to the shared bathroom along the landing, because it was just me and Mother. And there'd been a corresponding drop in her temperature.

'Oh, he's like *that*, is he?'

She turned her nose up as if I'd just done a dump in front of her.

'Is that a problem?'

The stench of a lifetime's '*when you think about what they do, it's disgusting*' was rising.

'And are you like that, then?'

By that juncture, I didn't much like *her*. I could never but *love* her. Hadn't she always been the best mother, better than all the others—after school always there, tea prepared, and when the table was cleared, homework laid out there, hadn't she always encouraged me to work harder, go further?

Until I went too far.

I answered, 'Yes.'

And that *yes* could never be unsaid.

Mother was sobbing and I was on the far side of the room, far from comforting, when Dad walked back in.

'What's going on?'

'Ask your son!'

101

'Graham…?'

The door was still open. I kept my mouth shut, so Mother spelt it out for everyone on the staircase.

'He's a pissing poofter!'

I could not have predicted my father's reaction.

'Whatever he is, he's my son and I'm proud of him.'

And he hugged me, properly, perhaps for the first time. I could not have known then that this emollient gesture augured all would be well in the future: that, in the fullness of time, Mother might even wear her best hat to my wedding—to another man. Not to the man who would hold me *that* evening. His embrace was some time coming. This was before mobile phones: I couldn't just SMS an SOS. I had to leave a note in Guy's pigeonhole, wait for him to finish rehearsing (the Cuppers thing) then down an obligatory drinkie with Lottie (the *Eagle & Child*, probably) before finally his knock put Moz out of his misery.

I am human and I need to be loved, just like everybody else does.

That night I knew I was.

By extension, back then, I felt more love from Guy's 'Mummy' than my own: my first meeting with the Terrys (laissez-faire in the way that only those who've never had a worry, not really, can be) couldn't have gone more knife-through-butterly. But then, it wasn't as though they were meeting their son's first boyfriend: he'd been out since age fourteen: there'd been a number before I came along. And Helena—all gamine chic and chunky 'ethnic' jewellery—had a way of making *everyone* feel special: me, the waiter serving us, the entire restaurant.

Wasn't she in…?

And isn't that the guy from…?

Teddy—whom, it's true, did have a certain *eau de camp* about him—regaled us with stories of his own Oxford days over brunch in *Browns*—which reminded him of the branch on St Martin's Lane, where he was then playing. To my relief (savings dissipating more swiftly than I'd been anticipating) they treated us. Then it was over to the bijou *Burton-Taylor Theatre* to see Guy's Pinter with Lottie (who swooned sycophantically over this visitation from a duo of theatrical deities almost on a par with those the theatre was named after) before the Terrys dashed back to town for their own curtains that evening, with a *you were marvellous, darling*.

And he was. I was proud. Wowed. As were the Cuppers judges: in their round-up of that first day of the competition they praised especially my boyfriend's *assured performance*. He gave another, I seem to remember, that evening. And after, his heartbeat boxing my ear, I worried how my own piece might be received the following afternoon.

'They'll love you,' he assured me. 'How could they not do?'

Each entrant had half an hour. Such was the volume of submissions, performances were spread over five afternoons. The majority were abridgements of scripts known and loved. I had opted for something original instead—juxtaposing Hamlet's soliloquies (*now to my mother: I will speak daggers to her*) and my own coming out story (*Mum, I'm gay*) with words underscored by the music of Morrissey (*I am the son and heir of nothing in particular*).

I thought it innovative.

Guy thought it *genius*.

The judges commended my *well-observed regional dialect*.

Retrospectively, I can see it was somewhat wanky and some

form of therapy, but at the time I saw only burning injustices. How dare a panel of posh students praise my accent, as if I'd had some agency in it? How dare a panel of straight students tell me they didn't have *any issue* with anyone being gay, so they didn't see *any need* to go on about it?

You know, some of Morrissey's utterances *are* true: we really do *hate it when our friends become successful*. At the end of the week, my *uncommon* mess was overlooked, but Guy's classic rehash got selected for a *Best-of-Cuppers* showcase. To make me feel better about this, Guy hinted it was only because a boy he'd fagged for at school was on the judging panel; for some, networking starts young.

In the *Eagle & Child* after that showcase, Guy and Lottie celebrated *Best Actor* and *Best Actress* prizes and were already planning their next performances.

'Look Back in Anger! You'll play Alison and I'll play Jimmy!'

Okay, I was emerald with envy—and Lottie was sound enough casting for middle-class Alison, fallen for the wrong man. But Guy as working-class hero, angry young Jim, railing against a system that I felt was still firmly entrenched? I'd like to believe I went to the bar for a packet of Mother's favourite Scampi Fries, opened them in the middle of the conversation and said *is it me, or does something smell fishy?*

I didn't, but I did begin thinking *I* had fallen for the wrong man. I found the rough-and-ready accent he affected in their *Hilary*-term production as comic as his imitation of Brenda's back in *Michaelmas* and, unable to suspend my beliefs any longer, I dumped him the day after it opened.

Guy,

Goodbye.

Graham

I can't remember the exact contents, but that was its essence. Pigeon-posted—an Oxbridge text message. After the show that evening, he showed up at my door again, note in hand.

'I don't understand.'

I just shrugged. It wasn't that Guy had changed, but that *I* had. Before Oxford, I'd not known what class was, or even that it existed. But once I'd experienced its system in action, I could not separate the man—the *gentleman*—from my resentment of the privilege he'd been born into. So Guy became collateral in my class battle.

Poor little rich boy, take that!

I can't pretend I didn't enjoy it. Or that it didn't make life a little awkward—us in the same college, in the same tutor group. Lottie took his side, of course—took me aside to tell me I was *a fool to just throw him away*. I gave *my* best Jimmy Porter and laughed in her face.

Fuck him! Fuck all of 'em! They'll never let me be one of 'em.

And I never have been. Although I am now pescatarian.

It's been some decades since I pulled the poker from my rectum and stopped despising where I come from, but I have never been one of the *common people* again. I am a class refugee; I declined the roles life offered me. I mean, if I'd wanted to go into the roofing trade I'd have had it made. Just like that. Just like Guy walked into that starring credit.

He's now on Mother's television, doing a bit of bodice-ripping. Typecast again. And because I still enjoy a frisson, I prod the husband (who's made himself *so* comfortable on the recliner he's now drooling over its red pleather.) *You're missing my first boyfriend.*

The husband says he's *handsome.* Dad says he *never liked him.* Mum says she's *not seen him in anything in a long time.*

Well, his acting was so wooden his career was soon coffined.

Me, I played the long game.

Mum is asking if we want anything more to eat. These days she's more cheese*boards* than cheesy Wotsits.

I tell her it's time for bed; tomorrow I've to be back to town… and back on set.

21

Fairy Story

This should be the busiest time, the City's sharp lines blurred by motion. But its streets straighten towards the horizon without interruption. Silence puddles on its pavements. Only a solitary set of footsteps splash as—face masked, hands gloved—a man hurries homeward with groceries. And from one of his windows, Phaeton watches.

He has one window with a view onto the apartments opposite, the boulevard below, some sky above, some trees in a row. The other window offers multiple views. Right across the City. Shocking images. And shocking statistics. Sound-tracked by shocked experts. How many *it* has taken. How quickly it's advancing. How long before life might be back in motion.

The time when Phaeton could share his air with other men now seems a dream. Now it's women who keep things going in the City of Perpetual Motion—rushing to work in the morning, rushing home in the evening. While men sit indoors, in fear of contagion.

The first case was a tragedy, a morbid curiosity. The City Corporation had sent one of their men to explore the woodlands beyond the horizon. The man returned with stories of wondrous resources, with plans for exploiting them to keep their City in motion… and with a strange sallowness of skin, of which no one thought anything more than that he'd simply caught some sun.

But like newspaper left out too long, his complexion kept yellowing, his body desiccating. No draught was deep enough for him. No potion could rehydrate him. He died the husk of a

111

man—a papery body-bag, crumpled and brown. The Citywide window had shown close-ups to everyone.

Then City Consultants reported that they weren't entirely certain whether the man was dead or in some way dormant, corpse or cocoon—strange sounds had started coming from within what was left of him. The Citywide amplified the noises for everyone—they sounded like something beating. A heart. Or a wing.

So the remains were kept under observation. And the City kept on moving.

Then there came a second man—with skin like parchment and a thirst there was no quenching. Then more of them—drying and dying. Sallow and shrunken and sequestered for observation—all of them men.

City Citizens began panicking. Rumours were flying, rumours and questions: Had the contagion come from the woodlands? How come it was so catching? And why had it only come for the men?

Male Citizens began retreating, only venturing to work in the morning then home in the evening. Phaeton was among them; he didn't want to die. But in others, the urge to live manifested differently—and they stayed out to play. Soon they were dying in such volume that there was no longer room to retain their husks for observation. By then, some time had passed without apparent changes to the cocoons, so the City Coroners gave orders to ditch them beyond the City's circumference.

To contain the contagion, men were advised to work from home. But even in incarceration, the City remained in motion—for if the City were to stop moving, *what then?* So everyone went on working as if nothing were happening, working harder than they'd ever done—there were more messages than there'd ever been, and more calls that needed answering. Phaeton was able—through the Citywide window—to keep connected with other men. And for a while, the experience was novel. Life seemed to settle.

Then Citizens started spotting them—fluttering about town, hanging out on tree limbs. They looked almost human, but bijou and be-winged: they were barely bigger than infants and naked as newborns, their skins all shades of the spectrum, eyes enlarged and opalescent. Some called them *Bugs*. *Fairies* was what stuck.

Phaeton hadn't believed it until he saw one. Not through his Citywide window—they could fake those views, he knew. But through his window onto the boulevard below.

There it perched in the branches of the closest tree—blue-bodied and tiny, two outsize appendages, bold as a butterfly's, sprouting between shoulder blades. It was just sat there—no need to be anywhere, do anything—wings flapping, fluorescing in the sunshine. *Probably drying them.* That's what the Citywide had told him. *After hatching, they flap their wings to pump blood to them and to shake off the moistness of the chrysalis.*

At first, the Citywide window had been aglow with theories on what they were and where they'd come from. Then the City Corporation made an announcement: the cocoons had begun to open and fairies were emerging. The men, not dead but dormant, were returning to life—and to the City—transformed.

And what a transformation. Fabulous as any drag queen sashaying across Citywide screens—day-and-night preening, partying, piss-taking. Throwing shade upon Citizens toiling beneath them. Citizens who looked up at them, looking out for lost loved ones—struggling to see some semblance of partners and brothers in these indolent creatures. *How dare they do nothing! In the City of Perpetual Motion!* Even more shocking than their inaction was their breeding.

Wings dry, the fairy in Phaeton's tree had wasted no time in pumping blood to another part of its anatomy. Its manner might be described as feminine, but it was clearly male in form. They were all quite clearly male in form. Including the second fairy who joined the first in Phaeton's tree. And right there and then, the two began to play.

Citizens were scandalised. Mothers covered children's eyes, dragged them from the obscenity. *How dare they! In our trees!* Phaeton though, had stayed at his window. It was the closest he'd come to any action in some time. He was pretty sure the fairies saw him. And that their look said *want to join?*

They were joined by more fairies every day, their numbers swelling slowly until a colourful colony swarmed above the City. Wherever fairies were found free-spiriting, the City Constabulary would threaten to arrest them. But those bug-boys just laughed and buzzed off: no one would spoil their fabulousness.

The City Councillors decreed there must be no more *homometaboly*: no more of their men transformed into fairies. Men must stay home: they would cook, care for children, and leave the house once weekly to do the shopping. But still the City must keep moving, so it was decreed that women would take over everything.

And so everything became, some argued, better run.

As a single man of twenty-one, the novelty of self-isolation has by now worn thin for Phaeton. His is a two-room, two-window home. It might have been okay if he'd had someone to share it with him, but he's not had human contact in... he forgets how long. He's felt no sensation unplanned from another's hand. Just his own, up and down. He's scoured the Citywide for stimulation, and scoured it again. That self-pleasuring, according to expert opinion, boosts the immune system is small consolation for boredom. Or depression.

One night, he dreams he's on a bike and his mother is pushing him. *Go on!* He wobbles into a green unknown. *Peddle or you'll fall!* He peddles. Doesn't fall. But the ground starts falling away beneath him. Down and down he's speeding. He can't stop feet or wheels from turning. His brakes aren't working and there's a ditch at the bottom that he's going to topple into, so he's screaming and screaming but no sound is coming…

He wakes with her voice still clear in his ear.

Useless, you are! Can't ride a bike without stabilisers!

He can't sleep, starts pacing. Around and around his apartment.

If I don't do something soon, then…

Eventually, his single-view window lightens. And there is the fairy, as every morning—looking like he's been up all night partying. Spotting Phaeton, he starts waving. And Phaeton waves shyly back at him. He decides it's time to go shopping.

'Hey handsome,' the fairy calls down, his voice countertenor and clear. Phaeton can't help smiling behind the mandatory mask he's wearing, as with gloved hands he locks the door behind him.

'Come up and see me some time,' the fairy calls when, bags in hand, Phaeton opens the door again. It's tempting to pull the mask from his mouth and flirt right back at him. But it wouldn't do for other men to see such a thing, as they stood at their windows, watching.

Back before the Citywide, Phaeton starts to explore some of

the more remote theories out there, one view leading to another.

They're getting it deliberately!

Having pupation-parties!

Fairies sow their seed in men and then it eats away at them!

To Phaeton, these fancies seem far-fetched, yet the experts remain uncertain how the contagion continues to spread.

That night he dreams he's cycling again. Down and down. About to hit bottom, Phaeton lifts his hands from handlebars to eyes, and instead of crashing starts to fly. Looking down, he sees his bike ditching and his mum pointing.

I knew it! He's one of them!

He wakes abruptly, sheets messy. It's dawn already. Looking out the window for his fairy, he finds the branch empty.

Probably breeding.

But next day the fairy is still gone.

Probably dead then.

They never lived long, these born-again men—their corpses blew all about town, wisps of things. Neither did they litter long; the women organised incineration teams. Paper-thin, the remains went up in seconds.

In the absence of his fairy, Phaeton feels lonelier then ever and seeks Citywide company. He gets talking to a vellum-skinned gentleman, who invites him to a party.

'What sort of a party?' asks Phaeton.

'Have you heard of pupation?'

It is true then.

Phaeton declines the invitation. But a can has been opened, and thoughts begin worming. *Does he want to live a caterpillar, sequestered in a glass jar? Or does he want to join the bug-boys and die a butterfly?* He's changing his mind about changing his body. He imagines his skin papering, his wings pullulating. And it feels so good to be something other than his present reduction, to be unlocked again.

He opens the Citywide window, closes it, opens it once more. Frames a message, reframes it. As soon as he sends it, he's regretful. And can barely contain his arousal.

The man gets back with details.

In the days following, Phaeton is still thinking *I might, I might not*. But on Saturday night, masked and gloved, he leaves his apartment under cover of dark. Hurries into the City Cab that pulls up. The driver is in on it; his windows are blacked.

'Alright, mate... Your blindfold's on the seat.'

The inhibition of vision had been a condition of acceptance: the host has to protect himself from potential repercussions.

'You won't need the mask and gloves where you're heading.' Another stipulation was the underwear, in which Phaeton sits sweating for what seems the longest time, a long winter coat his only other garment. 'You have reached your destination.' As the driver guides him out into the warm spring evening, Phaeton's anticipation is almost overwhelming.

He hears voices, a door closing behind him. His blindfold and coat are taken from him. The first thing he sees is the candelabra burning—flames down-lighting the gathering. To be in the same space as other men again, to be breathing the same oxygen, feels exhilarating.

The flat is not so much bigger than Phaeton's, but is *so* full of men.

Some of them have complexions already papering.

Some are still moist-skinned, like Phaeton—nervously nodding, uncertain of what's coming, enjoying the camaraderie of transgression.

Everyone is drinking. The host is flitting, refilling receptacles from a bottle of burnished liquid. More parched in the flesh than he'd appeared on Citywide, he is the heaviest drinker. Offering a glass to Phaeton, he explains, 'It's nectar.' Before Phaeton can ask any more, the host has flitted elsewhere.

Phaeton hesitates, raises the liquid to his lips. He has never tasted anything like it—so sweet he can but sip—bronze-bodied with a floral finish. And as the nectar takes its effect, his senses become amplified.

Background music becomes fore.

He becomes aware of his own odour. And that of the others.

Everyone wears only underwear. Everyone is on the dancefloor.

He joins them there, has no cares—the present is all that matters. Just to be there with those others who are not others—they're all in this together. He is in them, and they in him. None end, none begin.

A ripple spreads among them: *the fairies are coming.* Phaeton and the other fresh-skins are at the centre of its circle and open.

Candles are flickering above them; wings are fluttering.

Soon they would be beautiful as butterflies.

And soon they would die.

22

Beautiful Ones

The lights go down. In the auditorium, Steven checks the mirror behind the bar. He smooths side-swiped hair, swabs stray mascara, and tries to ignore the bowtie the theatre makes him wear. The audience start applauding, obscuring the exit music; never one to miss a whiff of Zeitgeist, Tom has gone for Suede's *Beautiful Ones*, its brazen optimism seeming to soundtrack this moment: soon there would be a new government.

And there he is as lights come up again, the man of the moment: not beautiful but handsome in that tux he's wearing, Tom steps from the baby grand, smiling as his nostrils catch the sweet smell of press-night success. His eyes seem to catch Steven's; Steven is smiling so hard it's hurting: that man up there is *his* man.

Then Tom's eyes move on: the maestro has been joined by his star. Julie is the beautiful one. Blooms that magically match her gown have materialised in her hands. The audience start whooping and soon will be swooping on the bar for the free wine Steven has laid out for them.

By the time all the reviewers have been replenished at least once—most often more—and air-kissed out the door by Dougie, the producer, by the time all their glasses have been rallied and rinsed and racked, Steven fears the party will be over. But from outside the dressing room, it sounds like they're still high-wired.

He knocks, adopts a nonchalant stance.

'Come in!' Dougie's voice comes back at him, his words with

always at least one extra syllable in them. As Steven codes the door open, Dougie is pouring champagne, his generous proportions all but obscuring the bottle in his hand. 'Darling, you're just in time!'

He slips a flute to Steven.

'Then this cock comes through the cubicle wall!' Tom is full-flow across the bijou dressing room. In light less flattering, his hair is thinning. Tux on railing, he's changing into something more casual and taking the opportunity to casually show his pectorals.

'No!' Julie is playing straight man, though she's actually a chain-smoking lounge-singing lesbian—lipstick now counterpointed by boots and jeans. It had been Dougie's idea to partner her with Tom for a *postmodern reinvention of popular songs*. It seems to be working.

Tom holds his hands pec-width to indicate the length of the aforementioned appendage. 'I'm not kidding.' He's trowelling on his thickest Lancashire accent.

'Darling, do stop bragging.' Dougie refills their glasses. 'There are children present.'

They like to remind Steven of the age difference: he's twenty-two; Tom is seven years older. He had been a visiting lecturer at drama college; Steven had been smitten and seduced in his final term. Then Tom got him the bar job on graduation.

Julie smiles sweetly-slash-smugly. 'Isn't he handsome in his uniform?'

Her vowels are purest Essex. Steven feels himself flush the same scarlet as his waistcoat.

'Oh-aye! The lesbian's for turning.' The man of the moment knows that girls who do boys like they're girls are all the fashion.

'Stick to the curtains, darling. Men are all beasts.' Dougie flutters eyelashes in Steven's direction. 'Present company excepted.'

'Cheers!'

'Cheers!'

'Cheers!'

'Well done.' Steven had loved it.

'So you liked it?' Tom doesn't need to be told that.

'I did.' Steven has to maintain *some* power in their relationship.

'That's all we're getting, obviously.' Tom swings the spotlight back his own way. 'Now, where was I?'

Julie is cued and ready: 'The cock was coming through the cubicle wall, I believe!'

As they slip back into their routine, Dougie sidles up to Steven.

'You don't get jealous?'

Before he'd even worked out he was gay, Steven had decided monogamy didn't work—certainly, it hadn't for his parents—so, of course, he couldn't give a shit how many 'cottages' his boyfriend frequents.

'Less for me to deal with.'

He is woken by a hand panning down his body. Last night they'd drunk too much to get anything up, so Tom has woken horny. Tom is *always* horny. Steven rarely initiates sex, but rarely resists when it's offered him. It's risky without a condom, but Tom had been insistent. They'd been seeing each other almost a year when Steven had surrendered. He's pretty certain that, with the others, a hand-job is as far as Tom ventures.

'That's better.' After, Tom spoons closer beneath the Heal's duvet cover.

Now it's over, Steven needs him out of there. 'Is it okay?'

'Bit pooey.'

Steven is on the toilet doing the necessary when Tom—never one for boundaries—squeezes by. 'I feel like shit,' he says.

'Yeah, you look it.'

'Ta.' Tom seeks a second opinion in the Habitat mirror: his bathroom may be bijou but the decor is impeccable.

'Better get moving—got an audition.' Steven's not had a gig since graduation; the casting is for an advertisement, but the pay is handsome. 'What you up to today?'

'Lying in the recovery position… See you after the show, then?'

'I think I might stay at mine tonight,' Steven says, flushing.

Steven spends most of his time at Tom's place, but has his own when he needs space. By the time the show comes down, the appeal of retreating alone to 'bedsitland' has waned somewhat, so he decides to try his luck on cuddles and cock.

He knocks at the dressing room door. No answer, no one there. Within, wilting flowers top-scent the air. Tom's tux adds a bass note; Steven inhales his man in absentia.

'Where are you?' Steven leaves through stage door, phone shouldered to ear.

'Went for a drink with Julie.' Tom is in a bar—gay, by the sound of the Kylie.

'Oh.'

'You didn't say you were coming, so…'

'Shall I come join you?'

'You could do…' Which means *no*. 'But to be honest, we're both feeling a bit post-press-night. I think we'll just have one and turn in.'

'Alright.' Steven resigns himself to the prospect of a single night in a single bed. 'Tomorrow I'm on matinee shift—I'll make food for when you get back.'

He's had a key since leaving drama school, staying at Tom's place in Notting Hill while he'd scoured *Loot* for something vaguely affordable within a mile or two. He lets himself in, puts down his shopping, peddle-bins his gum.

And spots the butt beside his foot.

Tom doesn't smoke; neither does Steven. The plot thickens.

On closer inspection, the butt exhibits a trace of scarlet lipstick.

The bass drops.

When Tom comes through the door, his favourite *Piano Man* is on the Bang & Olufsen, the wine is open and—with more energy than may be strictly necessary—Steven is grating parmesan. He surprises Tom with a kiss; he isn't usually so demonstrative, expressing affection more readily through the medium of cookery: he's made his boyfriend's favourite linguine.

'How was the show?'

'Storming. How was your audition?'

'That was yesterday, Tom.'

Not yet daring to dig into that cigarette end's origins, Steven digs pasta from the pan.

Tom has gone straight for the wine. And to the heart of the affair: 'Listen... Last night, Julie came back.'

'I know!' Steven turns his voice up to full brightness. 'She left her fag butt!'

Tom seems disarmed by this and takes another swig. 'We ended up having sex.'

A million disconcerting emotions pass through Steven as he

passes pasta from pan to plate. He permits Tom to see none of them: the show goes on. 'And how was that, then?'

'It was...' This probably isn't the script Tom has prepared. 'Well, it's been years since either of us...' He is clearly improvising. 'We had to work out how it all works, if you know what I mean. But then...'

Steven sets his smile, then the plates on the table. 'What?'

'It's nice to fuck something that's meant to fit your cock.'

A lifetime's self-hatred in a sentence; it gets to Steven, and with his back to Tom, he doesn't care if it's showing. All the same, he tries to keep his voice even. 'You going to do it again?'

'Don't know, probably. Is that okay?' Tom sounds stunned to be let off so lightly.

Steven suctions his safety-mask back on, turns.

'We'll have to have a threesome.'

Steven stalls inside stage door, delaying a backdraft of emotion: through safety glass he can see her, smoking. All evening, people have been weird with him. Like they know something they assume he doesn't. Like they're torn between feeling sorry for him and salivating over this new sensation.

A gay man and a lesbian! Imagine!

Steven is determined to get the joke on his own terms. Julie turns as he pushes the door open and steps into the ring.

Phase one: disarmament.

'Great show!'

Julie tightens her grip on the helmet in her hand, ready for battle.

'And great reviews!'

'Thank you. Tom's just coming. I...'

'I'm not looking for *him*.'

Phase two: seduction.

Julie hides her astonishment inside an exhalation, offers the packet to Steven.

'Why not?' He takes a cigarette.

She leans in to light it. Succeeds on second attempt.

'Thanks.' He holds her eyes. *Intense.*

'Hello!' Tom comes to Julie's rescue, another helmet in hand. 'You're smoking?'

Steven tries to keep down his inhalation. 'Thought I'd try one.'

'Ready then?' Julie stubs her Marlboro in the gutter.

'Have fun!' Steven's hopes disappear around the corner with them. He continues smoking as he listens to them laughing, then to her motorbike speeding into the London hum. The nicotine, kicking in, craves alcohol for company.

He can get at least two in before closing if he hurries.

Steven, who has only once felt the urge to take advantage of his open-relationship, has never had the urge to take anyone back to his bedsit. But that night—*fuck it*—he needs a fuck, and in the morning wakes fighting over a single duvet with a gentleman whose name he cannot remember.

What had he been thinking? *Thinning hair, beard brushed with silver…*

The resemblance stops there, doesn't go lower.

Some mornings later he's in bed again with the real thing, even initiates sex with him. His man. Except, really, he isn't. Steven can tell Tom's heart's not in it—even if his dick is—but is doing his best not to think about it, or who that dick has last been in, as he rodeos on top of Tom, his performance culminating in a

129

cum shot that very nearly blinds the man.

'Sorry.' Steven dismounts quickly, convulsing in that way he convulses when he's not sure whether to laugh or cry. Tom dries his eyes with the towel Steven hands him, doesn't dare open them. Steven takes this opportunity to pan his hands down Tom's toned body. Tom turns away from him, doesn't want to cum.

And Steven knows for certain then.

Blanketed in Tom's dressing gown, Steven perches in the open-plan kitchen—eyes watering as the heat of his body raises the latent scent of the man-who-is-not-his-man to his nostrils one last time.

Tom emerges from the shower with towel about midriff, smells something different. 'When did *you* start smoking?'

'I thought you liked it.'

Tom ducks the bullet. It hits the Smeg. As Tom aims for the Gaggia, Steven fires another.

'This isn't really working, is it?'

'No, I suppose it isn't.'

Tom refills the coffee machine. Knowing he won't witness it again, Steven finds the familiarity of this morning routine unbearable.

'I really love you.'

'You say that *now*.'

Now the gate is open, horse gone, Steven can't stop sobbing.

'Is this curtains then?'

'Let's leave it for a bit. See what happens.'

Blackness pours into Tom's cup. Steven will not be sugar on the side of it.

'No.' He stubs his cigarette out. 'Let's not.'

The rest of the run is like a form of self-harm, seeing the two of them—Julie and Tom—shining in the curtain-lights every evening. But Steven refuses to hand his notice in, or to pull a sickie even: the theatre belongs to him as much as them. It's some consolation when the show doesn't extend, isn't the *something for everyone* Dougie had planned; its last night tortoises around after an allotted three weeks. Somehow, Steven never meets either of them face to face.

But now Julie is outside stage door again, as if taking a last opportunity to taunt him. He hares straight past her, will *not* give her the satisfaction.

'I didn't ask him to leave you, Steven!'

He turns. She's delivered him his chance to deliver the line he's been rehearsing.

'You didn't have to—I mean, why would he want my shit on his dick when he can have your scarlet lipstick?'

If she's shocked, she doesn't show it, takes a drag on her cigarette.

'All those men—they didn't matter one bit. But you... I couldn't compete.' *Wrong equipment*, but more than that. 'It's not just sex, it's...'

Catching sight of Tom watching from the safety of stage door, Steven is thrown off-scent. On seeing Steven seeing him, Tom withdraws.

'A bit of fun.' Julie crushes her butt under boot, determinedly. 'Or it was meant to be.'

'Maybe for you. *He's* head over heels.'

She looks at him like this is news. But it was obvious to everyone: Tom had got off on the transgression, then had fallen for the woman. Steven stakes his claim on a sinking island.

'And he didn't leave me, I left him.'

Suddenly light snaps up on them.

'Everything okay?' Dougie is leaning from stage door, speaking to Julie like Steven isn't there. 'Darling, we're just pouring the champagne.'

'Steven was just leaving.' Her fourth wall has been rebuilt in seconds.

Dougie holds the door open just enough to let her past him. A sliver of his former soft spot falls on Steven.

'Bye-bye, darling.'

Then Dougie shuts the door firmly behind them. And Steven is swimming solo in the London hum. As he heads out into it, his head music begins.

Here they come, the beautiful ones...

Bring them on.

He hits Soho, beautiful as an open wound.

23

Chemistry Set

MR DARREN ANDERSON

V

MR ADAM REDFERN

DEFENCE STATEMENT

(a) The defendant pleads not guilty to the charge of sexual assault, facilitated by narcotics. The complainant and he engaged in consensual substance usage and sexual activity.

(b) The defendant denies luring the complainant to his home in order to take advantage of him. He denies administering to the complainant such quantities of substances as he knew would cause him to lose consciousness. He denies continuing to engage in sexual congress with the complainant after the realisation he was no longer conscious. He denies inflicting bodily

137

harm deliberately during the complainant's period of insensibility.

(c)   The complainant was fully aware of the nature of the social gathering and chose to attend of his own volition. He was responsible for monitoring his own intake of substances and chose to imbibe such volumes as resulted in his loss of constraint, control and consciousness. He consented to sexual activity with multiple partners throughout the event.

(d)   The injuries sustained by the complainant could be the result of activity engaged in with any partner during the course of the evening.

Signed: Adam Redfern
Dated: 4/5/15

WITNESS STATEMENT

1. I, Morris Williams, of 40 Queenstown Road, London declare the facts in this statement come from my own personal knowledge.

2. I have known Adam Redfern for a year or more. We're not friends, exactly: he's someone I see socially and have met principally at parties.

3. He invited me to a party at his home in Islington on 17th October 2014. As I remember, there were about ten of us there: most I knew from previous parties and some I'd not seen before.

4. Mr Anderson was one of the new faces. He seemed nervous, and seemed to have been drinking; when he walked in, I recall thinking 'looks like trouble: everyone knows you don't mix G with alcohol'.

5. He soon lost his inhibitions and appeared to enjoy being centre of attention: he's a handsome young man. I think it's safe to say most of the company were keen to have their way with him. And probably did at some point in proceedings.

6. Which is to say, things got out of hand: the injuries Mr Anderson sustained remain regrettable, but attributing individual blame seems impossible.

7. I believe the facts in this statement are true.

Signed: Morris Williams
Date: 5/5/15

MEDICAL REPORT

- Mr Anderson has inflammation and abrasions accompanied by bleeding on and inside the lips. A foreign object appears to have been inserted into the mouth. Swabbing has revealed traces of semen and faecal matter in the throat area.

- He has contusions on the torso, predominantly around the nipples, and more about the wrists, consistent with the usage of restraints. There are punctures to the skin of the left arm consistent with hypodermic injection.

- He has inflammation and abrasions accompanied by bleeding around the anus and inside the rectum. A foreign object appears to have been inserted into the anal canal. Swabbing has revealed traces of semen.

- Blood and urine samples have been taken to be tested for gamma hydroxybutyrate, methamphetamine and alcohol.

Signed: Dr N. Ramasamy
Date: 18/10/14

WITNESS STATEMENT

---

1. I, Leanne Sansom, of 17 Bradford Street, London declare this statement is true, to the best of my knowledge.
2. I met Darren on our Hairdressing and Barbering NVQ in 2011 and we've been best friends since then. Last year, we moved into a flatshare together.
3. I now work at Sassoon and—since Darren started at The Grooming Lounge—we always meet in the West End for drinks on Friday evenings. Unless one of us has a date or something. But on Friday 17th October 2014 he said he couldn't meet me and was secretive about why. Usually we tell each other everything—I always say Darren knows more about me than any man. When I asked if I could come, he said he was going to a party and it wasn't for women. I told him to be careful and take condoms. I wanted a full report as soon as he got home.
4. When I got up next morning Darren still wasn't in. I thought, *he must have had a fun night*. About ten o'clock I heard the door going and called out, 'What time do you call this then?' He wanted to go straight to his room. I could tell just by looking at him something was wrong. When I asked what, he started crying.
5. He didn't want to go to the police at first because he'd been taking drugs. I told him he couldn't get done for drug taking, only supply or possession. I couldn't believe he'd let the guy slam him. We go to the clinic together

141

every six months and he's a right baby when he has to get bloods done. That morning there was blood all over his Aussie Bums.

6.   I hate police stations. But the woman who dealt with us was brilliant—didn't bat an eyelid when she took the details down. My eyes were watering—imagine coming round to find someone's forced their forearm in. She sent him for examination.

7.   The clinic gave him something so he wouldn't get HIV, and tests for the other STDs. He had chlamydia but was otherwise 'all clear'. The mental damage is taking longer. He's not been out for a drink or date in forever.

8.   I believe the facts in this statement are true.

Signed: Leanne Sansom
Date: 1/5/15

VICTIM PERSONAL STATEMENT

I understand that the information contained herein on the extent and seriousness of the crime as it has affected me will be presented to the court on my behalf, and shall be considered by the judge at the time of sentencing the offender.

I've always been comfortable in my own skin. Unlike some guys, I never had any issues with my sexuality. My school and family were accepting and I've been out since I was sixteen. Since the assault, that's changed.

I rarely go out these days. I've tried to go out with guys. I can't relax with them. Everyone's noticed the change, even my clients. I only recently started working again. At first, I couldn't bear to touch even another guy's hair. I used to love being a barber.

I don't like talking about it to anyone. I feel ashamed. Like I'm to blame. If I hadn't got the app, if I hadn't replied to his messages, if I hadn't accepted his invitation then none of this would have happened. But he was so handsome and he made everything sound so exciting. He knew I was nervous of needles but said he'd look out for me, that I would be fine. He knew it was my first time. At a party like that, I mean. I'd heard about them but hadn't ever been invited to one. Now I wish I never had been.

My counsellor says I need to stop thinking like that, that I need to stay present. And I do try not to keep going back to it. But sometimes I have nightmares that it's happening again. I wake up imagining I'm surrounded by them, that they're tearing me open. Which is, basically, what happened. I came around to this incredible pain. I've never felt anything like it before and never want to again. I couldn't work out what they were doing. And then, when I did work it out, I couldn't do anything to stop them. It's like when you're dreaming—you can see a door but you can't push it open. My doctor's given me sleeping tablets. They help a bit. But I can't wait for the whole thing to be over and done. Then I'll feel I can move on.

It all just keeps going round and around. How did it go so wrong? I was having such a good time. He was right, it was exciting. And he seemed nice as well as handsome. So why did he do those things? I don't want him to be able to do them to me or anyone ever again.

Signed: Darren Anderson
Date: 1/5/15

Lucre Centre
Canada Square
London E14 5BL

30/4/15

To Whom It May Concern,

I am writing this reference in support of Adam Redfern and speak on behalf of his employer. I am Global Quality Manager, Equities Risk & Derivatives, at Lucrebank, a position I've held for the past five years. Prior to which, I was QA Manager at Lucre and Senior QA Analyst with Credit Norse. I live in London with my wife and our two children.

I have known Adam as an employee for two years. He joined us as a promising graduate in summer 2013 and very quickly became an invaluable member of the team. He's ambitious and hardworking: I did not hesitate to recommend him for promotion. Although I rarely make it to the pub myself these days, I've heard from colleagues he can also be extremely good company. Certainly, he is much-loved by everyone. It was therefore with some shock and disbelief that we learned of these allegations—which seem so completely out of character.

Of course, we knew of Adam's sexuality. Lucre pride ourselves on diversity: one of the senior team is gay, and my wife and I were delighted to attend his wedding (to his charming husband) recently. We also knew Adam liked to party: there were some Monday mornings when he did look like he might have been 'burning the candle at both ends', but this never got in the way of his working. It was also not—shall we say—unusual among

145

younger employees: financial services are a work-hard play-hard sort of industry.

When Adam came to me to report the case he was—to his credit—nothing but candid. And contrite: both for any inconvenience he could be causing the company, and for any distress he may have caused another gentleman. He was certain the claim was a matter of misunderstanding and I do not hesitate to believe this: I know Adam to be someone of great integrity, with a great career—and life—ahead of him.

I am, of course, happy to be contacted to verify the authenticity of this reference or clarify its contents. I'm certain it won't come to sentencing, but I would hope that Adam's always previously good character would be taken in to account by the Court under such circumstance.

Yours faithfully,

Murray Preston-Jones

23 Downsview Avenue
Rochester
Kent ME1 2SJ

HMP Belmarsh
Western Way
London SE28 0EB

30th May 2015

Dear Adam,

Sorry it's taken so long to write—there never seems to be a moment. I'm looking after the little one now your sister's back to work again and this time of year there's all the bedding plants to get in. Two hundred marigolds we counted! Your Dad's still at it. My eczema's been playing up, always does when I'm stressed, so I've come in to get the dinner started and left him to it. That and Janice came out to 'prune her privet'. You know what she's like—always wants to get her nose into everything. Always wants to know how you're doing up in London. And I'm afraid I couldn't face it. Not yet. Not that I'm going to tell her anything. I've told your father not to say a word to anyone.

When they read out the verdict, I couldn't believe it. Still can't. I don't think I stopped crying the next day. Little Liam kept asking me, 'What's wrong, Nanny?' Of course, I didn't tell him. But his mother knows everything, says she doesn't want you coming near her son. Which I can understand—because I'm not sure I want you coming near *any* of us again.

I remember thinking *what is it this time*, when you said you had to tell us something. When you told us you were gay it was difficult enough, but I've had to get used to that. Your auntie says I must have been the only one who didn't see it. I suppose it was staring me in the face, really—you were always such a gentle boy. Which is why it's so hard to imagine you doing what they said you did. It turns my stomach just to think about it. You weren't brought up like that! Why on earth would you want to do such things to that poor young man?

Your father always says, *don't ask the question if you don't want to know the answer*. Looks like he's finished the front border so I had better go check on that chicken. I hope you're eating. Do they do vegetarian in prison? I would say I'd bring you something, but I don't know if we'll be visiting. I don't know if I'll be writing again.

Yours sincerely,

Mum

Tuesday 18 Oct 2015

The Custodian

Opinion
Sex, Drugs & Parole

Polly Paterson

Being gay isn't all rainbow confetti—this perfect storm of chemistry, technology and sexuality is the legacy of our prejudices

So we (finally) have gay marriages, and just when Middle England thought it safe to peg freshly-laundered LGBTs on the line with the rest of their white-washing, a new phenomenon has reared its head over the privet hedge. Dubbed *chemsex*, it's a variation on a perennial theme: getting high and laid at the same time. *Sounds like fun, right?* No wonder The Daily Filth have got their knickers in a twist.

Participants are almost exclusively gay men. Gay men with smart phones. Party invites don't arrive on doormats but via hook-up apps. Cocktails are sipped, snorted or injected. Crystal meth, GHB and mephedrone are the classic ingredients. Cue disinhibition, and all manner of sexual shenanigans—with multiple partners over multiple days. Poor old Profumo must be spinning in his grave.

149

Public Health England describe the situation as a 'ticking time-bomb'. It doesn't take Marie Curie to work out why: a bunch of guys throw precaution to the hurricane and—*wahey!*—gonorrhea, syphilis and HIV have a field day. Then there are the long-term mental health conditions waiting in the wings. *Would Sir prefer his trauma in psychosis or paranoia?* Oh, and did I mention that police are reporting an eye-watering *doubling* of chemsex-related crime so far in 2015?

Chemsexers are likely to be affluent and professional—not at all your typical 'drug-losers'. Men like Adam Redfern, a former fund manager now detained at Her Majesty's pleasure, after his conviction for narcotic-related sexual assault of another gentleman. So how do respectable, successful young men end up committing such crimes? Any GCSE psychology student might point you in the direction of self-esteem.

Pretty much every gay boy with whom I've ever been dancing—and there have been a fair few of them—has confessed, after a third gin-and-slimline, that their balletic bravura just *may* be the by-product of growing up feeling inferior to their straight peers. So is it any wonder such men take with aplomb to behaviours which make them feel like a queer King Kong – right down to plummeting-from-skyscraper ending?

Now, I've done some stupid things in my time, including the ingestion of some not entirely establishment-approved substances. But the chemsex phenomenon is something altogether different. Back when I was a chicken, raves were the big thing. The 'powers that be' weren't any fonder of them—but the arrests made back then were for trespass, not rape. Taking ecstasy (originally dubbed 'empathy') was all about going out and getting in a big warm bath with the rest of humanity—come one, come all (if you'll excuse the pun). These new drugs are about staying in and do not always seem to encourage fellow-feeling. *Consent anyone?*

The solution, obviously, is that LGBT-inclusive relationship education in schools should be obligatory. And MDMA must be available on eBay. Who knows, it may even help certain members of our cabinet to locate their all-too-obviously missing capacity for compassion.

HMP Belmarsh
Western Way
London SE28 0EB

23 Downsview Avenue
Rochester
Kent ME1 2SJ

13th May 2016

Dear Mrs Redfern,

I write to you in my capacity as prison chaplain. I understand there has been no communication between you and your son, Adam, since shortly after his incarceration; it will therefore come as something of a shock, I imagine, to learn that he has been referred to my care after an attempt on his own life last year. I would like to assure you he is now in sound physical health and is showing signs of recovering his former self. He has consented to my writing this letter on his behalf.

On our first meeting, I found Adam reluctant to engage with me and—when he did—he made it quite clear he has no faith. I, in turn, made it clear to him that my role within the prison is—these days—principally pastoral: I have no mission to convert inmates to the Christian faith. Or any other, for that matter. I am however, someone to whom prisoners can talk, simply on a human level. And that—should he wish to speak—I would listen without judgement.

It was with pleasure that I discovered that your son had requested a subsequent meeting. He has since responded enthusiastically to the opportunity to talk freely and it has been an honour to come to know him. As you will no doubt know, your son is an intelligent and sensitive man. The prison regime is not easy for anyone but seems to have been particularly hard on him. As has also, I glean, what he describes as your 'disowning' of him.

Adam is a complex character, and I suspect that he has not always been able to show the love that it is obvious (to me) he feels for his mother. I understand that when he was a child the two of you were close but grew apart in his adolescent years. You may or may not know that Adam was badly bullied at school during that time, but he never felt able to tell his family about it. That abuse was homophobic and it is apparent that his sexuality has been difficult for both him, and for you, to come to terms with.

Adam tells me you are a believer and—as one woman of faith to another—I assure you that I believe that *gay* is how God intended your son to be. Of course, I appreciate fully that the nature of his crimes may be much harder to accept than his sexuality. Indeed when first convicted, Adam himself found great difficulty in countenancing his own culpability, to the extent that he was in denial of even having committed a criminal act. And sadly, once he had accepted that fact, he found it impossible to reconcile himself with it.

He has now been with us almost a year and, I am told, has made significant progress in that time. He has shown compassion for the victim. And also for himself: he realises he may have been acting out repressed feelings of disempowerment and self-hatred, and is intent that these should never manifest in such a manner again. In short, there has been sufficient positive advancement for him to be considered a viable candidate for early release.

But at a recent meeting, Adam expressed indifference to the possibility of parole. Responding to my questioning over this, he claimed it didn't much matter to him if he was inside or 'out there'—he no longer had anything to go back *for*. He feels that he has lost everything—and now has no home, no job, no family, and no friends. This, in a way, is unsurprising. Such expressions of pessimism about facing the outside world again are not uncommon: inmates often find the prospect of release overwhelming. I encouraged him to consider possible positives—the opportunity to make new friends, for instance. He seemed uncertain as to how this could happen, when everything he did would be monitored—online and off—and when he was allowed out, he'd have to wear a tag.

At that point, I suggested re-establishing contact with you, as a parent's unconditional support can often be an invaluable part in the rehabilitation process. He wouldn't hear of it, reasserting you didn't want *anything to do* with him. I suggested he allow me to write, a service chaplains can undertake when we deem it appropriate. This possibility he also rejected.

But before our meeting that day finished, we had rather a personal exchange. I should explain that I am presently expecting my first child, and Adam enquired about the due date, which I gave to him. He asked if it was a boy or a girl, and I explained that we were waiting for the birth to find out the child's biological sex. Adam reflected on this, and then asked me to promise that the child would grow up knowing it was loved, whatever it was... and *for* whatever it was.

I don't mind admitting, I found myself crying as the door shut behind him.

At our next meeting, he assented that I should have your

address—a sign, perhaps, that I have gained his trust. And also that he is aware I will soon start maternity leave. So now I appeal to you—as a mother and as a Christian—to love your son for what he is, and forgive him for what he has done wrong. It is now time for this young man (and at twenty-three, he is still so very young) to stop being defined by his crime and to start moving on. His passage back into the world will not be an easy one. But you could help him—in his own way—to be reborn.

Yours sincerely,

Chaplain Sarah Morgan

23 Prospect Rise
London E17 3EQ

16th August 2015

Dear Mum,

I just wanted to drop you a card to say thank for meeting me. It was lovely to see you again, even if it was difficult to talk properly at the station café.

I thought you might appreciate the print on the front of this: it's Marigold by William Morris. The house he lived in is now a museum and garden just up the road from here: maybe next time you come up we could go there.

Love,

Adam

x

24

A Bigger Universe

'I believe we have a duty to do the right thing.'

Fuck.

'Getting the debts and the deficit under control has to be done.'

Fucking David Cameron.

'But I also have a burning mission to build a bigger society…'

Fuck off! Bryann silences the radio alarm and sinks into sleep again. By the time they resurface from slumber, they've only ten minutes to get there.

'FUCK!'

The February air is a bucket of water as they fling back the covers, fling an outfit together from whatever's on the floor, and fling themself from the door.

'FUCK!!'

Their bike has a puncture.

'FUCK!!!'

The bus pulls off just as they reach the stop. And the next one sits forever in a single-file of single-occupancy cars, as another privatised operation disfigures another public thoroughfare. Roadworks be damned, they demand the driver release them and run the final furlong (in three-inch platforms, easier said than done).

'You are late,' says Al-Assad on the door.

'A few minutes.' (It's half an hour.)

'You will receive a letter.' He black-marks their name.

'It's not Bryan; it's Bry*ann!*' Doors swinging shut behind them, they sashay from the Jobcentre 'saloon' into the wilds of West London.

A Bigger Building Society

Bryann pounds pavements home, putting the pound saved from bus-fare towards tobacco and papers. Outside the shop on the corner, dark clouds gather but do not dare shower before Bryann is through the front door.

On decrepit carpet, a letter. Teal-nailed, they tear into the envelope on the stairs. Reading the header, they realise it's addressed to Mr McDonough. But he's dead, so who cares?

Annual summary statement: twenty-two thousand, two hundred and seventy-two pounds and twenty-four pence.

So he'd had money, the old git... And in two years, no one had claimed it.

In 2008—three years earlier—the flat on the first floor was still two bedsits and *they* was still a *he*, twenty-one and fresh-faced from university. The ad had said studio apartment. It was ten by eight. The kitchen was a cupboard with sink and cooker. *The glamour*. But it was central, and affordable on Bryan's wages as a waiter; he'd put in an offer.

The landlady had taken his deposit. Then taken him to meet his new neighbour. Inside the front door to the flat was a small hall with three more doors: Bryan's new bedsit, a bathroom (shared), and a third, on which she'd knocked.

'Who's there?' a querulous voice had called through the door, and then a pair of old eyes had peered through the crack that appeared.

As introductions were made, Bryan waved (not *too* limp-wristedly) from behind Mrs Masari.

'Mr Reeves here,' she boomed to Mr McDonough, still sheltering behind his door, 'will be giving you ten pounds every

Monday for electricity.'

Because they also shared a pre-pay meter.

Nightmare.

The next year was spent wrangling over whether it cost more to wash Bryan's (growing) hair or to feed Mr McDonough's heater.

That heater now sits starving in the corner. But the idea of *twenty-two thousand, two hundred and seventy-two pounds and twenty-four pence* warms Bryann's (light) fingers.

And—for the first time in some time—they're smiling.

All those letters to Mr McDonough they'd thrown unopened in the recycling… But now the Universe has intervened, setting a goldmine beneath them at just the right moment.

Universal Credit

A few days later, the letter is still sat by their laptop—its figures white-and-black fact, but as yet unassailably abstract. Clouds (black) are again amassing, and a bitter wind blowing but, woollened and wadered, Bryann has ventured online in the hope of landing *something* from that day's no-to-low-pay castings (actors, it seems, can live on nothing but acclaim).

When Mr McDonough had (finally) passed on, Bryann had taken the whole flat on; they'd been having a good run. A transfer to the West End, some bit parts on television—their career was sailing in the right direction. But then they'd hit the dole-drums—a turnaround possibly not unrelated to the *pioneering* decision to change name and pronoun. Their agent had tried to dissuade them, but Bryann was determined—*no more appeasement of the gender-polar system!*

They are now typing a letter of appeasement (for the social security system). It does not come any more naturally to them than conforming to male or female norms.

Dear Sir slash Madam (slash Human Being),

Please give me this job I do not want and for which I am only applying so the cowhands in the Jobcentre Saloon can put a tick in a box and gold-pan their statistics. Please find enclosed my CV: I am prodigiously overqualified, as you can see.

Yours faithfully…

They needn't have bothered. In the hall downstairs, they find the letter promised by Al-Assad of the Jobcentre.

Dear Jobseeker,

We have looked at your claim and cannot pay your allowance any more. We cannot pay you because you have had three consecutive warnings for late attendance, so we have struck you from our list to gold-pan our statistics. If you want to know more about this decision please contact us and we will give an explanation.

Lots of love,

The Government Goldmining Corporation.

Back upstairs, Bryann paces from one room to the other, phone pressed to ear. A voice recording: feelings decompressing. A list of options: black bile rising. A synthesized aberration of Pachelbel's *Canon*, then: 'I'm sorry, sir (*sir!*) there is nothing to be done. Please fill in form GL24 if you think our decision is wrong.'

Cue eruption.

Cunts!

The phone is propelled across the room; cloud obscures everything.

Why did they not get out of bed on time?

namaste /ˈnʌməsteɪ/ exclamation

They've still not learnt to see it coming. Or, they've still not learnt to admit they see it coming—a connection broken between sense and brain. But they *have* learnt how to keep going—how to place a foot down, and then the other one—even when *nothing* can be seen. Some cigarettes and sun salutations later, a chink in cloud-cover—*et voila!*—enlightenment.

In the dressing-up box, Bryann finds mackintosh and flat cap. A touch of make-up, bend at the waist, quaver in the voice. (A drama school training comes in useful sometimes.)

And, rehearsal:

(Mssr McDonough steps up to the counter.)

Can I help you, sir? (They'll let the *sir* pass as they're in character).

Yes, please. You see I've lost my passbook. Can't think where I put it. But I have got this annual summary statement.

No problem. How much would you like?

All of it.

And how would you like it?

Quick.

(She reaches under the counter, and then counts the money out before her.)

Now, if you could just sign here…

A signature—why had they not thought of that before?

They scour through drawers, sure they had it somewhere.

They made him sign to say they'd given him money for the meter!

They scour drawers once more, catch themself in the mirror. The cap, the mac, the make-up—they look ridiculous. And then they see themself on a surveillance monitor (unflatteringly lit,

165

somewhat blurred).

That is *me at the counter, Your Honour.*

And then in artist's impression (nose somewhat disproportioned) as the judge pronounces sentence.

Is fraud an imprisonable offence?

Clouds loom like rent payments; the money returns to abstraction; the Universe says *try again.*

Online Wanking

Next morning, they force themself up (one foot, the other foot); and while typing their constitutional on Facefuck (Liberty! Equality! Non-Binary!) another idea lights up, lifts gloom.

What if they did it online?

No forgeries. No disguises.

Bryann flip-flops the statement, and there it is.

You can manage your money how, when, and where you choose with our internet banking service.

They type in the address.

Register

Click.

I want to register my…

Savings account.

Account number

0321/482559464

First name

Frederick

Surname

McDonough

Postcode

W10 6SR

Date of Birth…

Damn.

They can picture the medical card in their hand, can remember thinking *that makes him eighty-something.* The meter had run out of money and, needing the key, they'd pounded on the door, but Mr McDonough wouldn't open up, wouldn't answer, and they couldn't even hear him in there, hadn't heard him in over twenty-four hours. So they'd called the police, who came and could *smell something*, said *better not look this won't be pleasant*; proceedings were possibly worse in Bryann's imagination as the police broke the door down. The old man was unconscious on the floor, shit everywhere. Bryann had searched decay-scented drawers for the meter key and there was nothing, almost nothing, to see but some yellowing underwear and the medical card with the name of Mr McDonough's doctor, which they gave—along with their number—to the two handsome ambulance men who came, flashing and screeching to stretcher out the old man, an Egyptian queen.

He must have been born in nineteen twenty-something…

But an exact date eludes Bryann.

Lightning; eviction, destitution, prostitution in flash-frame; the Universe shrugs a shoulder, says *try harder.*

Personal Debit

They only saw Mr McDonough once more: the next day the hospital had rung to request the old man's dentures: could Bryann have a look for them? They *supposed* that would be possible. The door was still broken, carpet still stinking; they'd tried not to touch anything. Not that there was much to touch—the chest of drawers, an armchair, a single bed—beneath which they found the false teeth. They wrapped the discoloured set in plastic, washed their hands in antiseptic. Later, en route to the theatre, they took a detour; the nurse told them that they'd been *Freddie*'s only visitor.

In that ward full of geriatric gentlemen and their concerned children, he did look very alone. He slipped the dentures in, dust still on them, and smiled at Bryann, perhaps for the first time.

'Where'd you find them?'

'Under your bed,' Bryann shrugged.

Freddie frowned. 'You been beneath my mattress?'

Bryann shook their head with a vigorousness which seemed to pacify their neighbour; he beckoned them closer.

'Lift the bottom corner. You'll find a fiver,' he whispered. 'You done me a great favour.'

In a household of silent men and scornful women, Bryann had learnt young to keep emotion hidden, storing it away to discharge subsequently on stages and screens. Flushing with feeling (and being then flush) he said:

'I don't want your money.'

Freddie seemed disturbed by the concept of being in someone's debt and sought another way to balance the sheet.

'Then will you have some tea, at least?'

Bryann had to be at work by six for warm-up: they kept watch on the clock as they sipped tepid liquid from a mug the nurse had been entreated to bring. For a year, Bryann and the old man had lived like odd shoes in a box—Freddie knowing nothing of his neighbour's life and Bryann knowing nothing of his. They learnt something of it in those fifteen minutes, not all of it coherent—Freddie McDonough had grown up in Belfast and *may* have been in the army. If there had ever been wife or children, there was no mention of them. Bryann can remember thinking *don't let this be me in sixty years' time.* No flowers, no fruit. No one to whom they might bequeath their life savings.

They'd resolved then and there to accept the request on Facefuck from that banker-with-biceps: *loved you in that Channel Four thing—can I take you to dinner sometime?*

Some days later, over starters, their phone had broken the atmosphere. They knew it had to be important as the landlady was too tight to call a mobile usually (and the banker was boring them, anyway). They made their apologies.

On leaving the hospital that afternoon, Bryann had told Mrs Masari about the situation. Now, she told Bryann that Freddie had died that morning. And still, no one had been to visit him. Bryann was surprised to feel saddened that the hospital had reached out to her and not them.

But then…

A certificate of death would give a date of birth.

Sunshine, songbirds, accolades; Bryann *throws shade* on the Universe.

Life Cycle

General Register Office

Click.

Order certificates online

Click.

If you are using the site for the first time you will need to complete the registration.

Fuck.

These details will be used to determine the delivery address for any orders you may place…

169

…and to determine the guilt in any offence you may commit.

Bryann's fingers start back from the trackpad, leave no print.

Rain spits; their reputation is in bits; the Universe says *maybe you should try something different?*

They keep on searching.

You can order certificates through the General Register Office or from the local authority where the event took place.

The hospital was in Westminster.

We hold records of births, deaths, and marriages that took place in the City of Westminster from 1837 to the present. Certified copies of entries from these registers may be produced, provided that all required information can be supplied—such as the name of person(s), date, and place of event.

A scroll through Bryann's Facefuck timeline yields a picture of them and banker-with-biceps, candlelit in that priceless-but-tasteless restaurant. 20th February 2009.

You can obtain a copy by post or in person.

In the latter case, they won't have to provide a postal address.

To apply in person, please visit our offices during working hours (Mon-Fri) along with your completed application form and the appropriate fee.

Speculate to accumulate.

A standard certificate costs £9.00.

Tobacco shall be rationed.

Orders received before 1pm can be collected the same day. Download and print our application form below.

They'll cycle over tomorrow.

A revival; a rainbow.

they /ðeɪ/ *pronoun* [singular & plural]

Just before 1pm, under severe strip-lighting, Bryan hands over a completed form with a composure that can only be acquired at RADA. The registrar is now holding enough evidence to file for prosecution: false name, false address, false signature. *Relation to deceased:* great nephew (eyeroll). *Reason for request:* tracing family tree. She doesn't ask for ID but does ask for the fee. They pay cash, obviously. She tells them to return at 3.30.

It's an unusually warm February afternoon; they walk while they wait. Regent's Park. A smoke by the lake—water sparkling in spring-like sun. Ebbing with each exhalation, yogically flowing. The Universe in motion. And they are a permeable membrane; there is no separation between the Universe and them. They lose themself for a moment and do not hear her approaching.

'Spare a cigarette?'

She is in drab from head to toe, shrunken as a sparrow.

Bryann shakes their head. 'Sorry.' They've almost nothing left.

Her eyes tell them that it's what she was expecting. Her resignation breaks Bryann.

'Here, have it.' They offer her the packet, lighter to go with it.

Slice-of-lemon teeth cleanse the palette of her face.

'I appreciate it.'

And her happiness is theirs; blue sky everywhere.

Charity Begins at Home

They open the envelope in the town hall toilets. Scan the certificate. *Frederick McDonough. Born 16ᵗʰ May 1927, Royal*

Jubilee Hospital, Belfast. Died 20th February 2009, St Mary's Hospital, London.

Win, win; it's him.

Emerging onto the Marylebone Road, Bryann is accosted by a gentleman.

'Have you got a moment?'

The bright bonhomie (and brighter finery) give his game away.

They would never stop, usually. Something stops them today. 'Okay.'

It's not the answer the rep has come to expect. 'Oh, so… How are you?'

They go off-script completely. 'All the better for seeing you, obviously.'

The rep *is* cute, but straight. 'Anyway, I'm working for a charity…'

'Oh, I see. I thought you just wanted to talk to me.'

He's gone as red as his jacket. 'Well, I do but…'

Or maybe he's just *heteronormative.*

'So, if I give you my direct debit, can you guarantee it'll all go on good causes and not your CEO's wages?'

'I…'

'Didn't think so. Bye now!'

He calls after them. 'But you could give me your details anyway?'

They cycle back. *Why not?*

'Bryann Reeves. B-r-y-a-*double*-n. Hit me up on Facefuck.'

Bryann rides into the sunset, stops at an internet café (no traceable IP), and spends the change from the registrar's fee. They input the necessary names, numbers, memorable data, and like Ali Baba, the bank unwittingly outputs a passcode (to arrive by post within five working days).

A starry canopy; they are legendary; namas-*fucking*-te.

Divine Non-Intervention

One week later, the code has still not appeared.

There's a storm blowing up, a whopper!

Cue paranoia.

Sudden activity after several years' dormancy?

Looks like fraud—computer says *no code.*

But what is the Universe saying?

Bryann can hear nothing except their stomach grumbling: they are living on a packet of gram flour and such condiments as the fridge can muster.

Chickpea-cleanse your chakras—feel a million dollars!

They feel like shit; they see it approaching:

A twister! It's a twister!

They can do nothing. And like in a dream, they cannot move and they cannot scream. Then it's upon them, the ground far beneath them; their thoughts are spinning.

Why did you stay in bed so bloody long?

They have seven pounds in pocket, six in bank.

Why did you not stay with that banker, you wanker?

Withdrawal of one benefit has precipitated a claim chain-reaction.

Why did you give your last tobacco to that fucking woman?

The worst withdrawal of all is from nicotine.

It's like that last West End curtain all over again—soaring one second, spiralling as job offers refused to roll in, then tumbleweeding to the jobcentre saloon to open a claim.

And now it's curtain up on the theatre of blame:

Why do you insist on self-sabotaging?

For encore, their father on the touchline:

Why can't you be a proper man?
Their mother down the phone-line:
When will you stop all this nonsense and get a proper job, son?
The Universe is still saying nothing.

One foot, then the other one—like the therapist told them. Before Bryann will return to the doctor for another prescription (and return to waiting tables in another restaurant), they will first return to the café, braving the wind's buffeting to gamble one last coin on requesting the passcode again.

They doomscroll the remainder of their paid-for hour: so-and-so's in this, so-and-so's doing that, and oh—the charity rep has sent a Facefuck request.

His profile pic is hot. And sweet.

Accept. Message:
Well, you took your time about it.
Silence, stillness, sepia.
Then the rep is typing:
Well, hello there!
Through a crack in the door, sudden technicolour.

Stella(r)

They run downstairs as soon as they hear the letterbox; the code is on the doormat. Back in the café that afternoon, the bank fires up a series of hoops.

Ring One! Customer Number!
They type in digits; the bank applauds and raises the next.
Ring Two! Memorable Date!
Of birth, of course.
Ring Three! Memorable Place!
Belfast.

Ring Four! Memorable Name!

Mary.

Ring Five! Pass Number!

Bryann copies it in, holds their breath, and then hits return.

Twenty-two thousand, two hundred and seventy-two pounds and twenty-four pence materialises before them in *pixel* rather than *paper* form. They scroll every option, click every button, hit return so many times in succession that the guy behind the counter shoots a warning, and yet *still* the money remains an abstraction: no cash-card can be ordered, no funds transferred.

Thunder, flame fountains; you brought the witches broom, but still you can't go home.

The Universe peaks from behind the curtain—*I did try to tell you, Hun.*

Oh, so that's where you've been hiding?

Always been here—you just wouldn't listen.

They're about to say something cutting, when they hear another voice saying:

'This government is not just making cuts, sitting back and saying *let's hope society steps forward*.' Fucking David Cameron. 'That's why we're establishing the Big Society Bank.'

The counter-guy is now watching television.

'The Big Society Bank will be funded by money from dormant accounts.'

Accounts like the one open (but *closed*) before Bryann.

'The bank's mission is to create a *sustainable social investment market*.'

Four words never before heard together. There are another four words on a board behind the counter: *staff needed apply here.*

Sign that it's time to test the *employment market*—start a new career as a data barista?

Bryann snorts. Counter-guy shoots another look.

The balloon takes off without them; the Universe waves a wand.

Are you ready now?

If the Universe thinks they're gonna just tap heels together and happily-ever-after, then the Universe has another thing coming. 'Home' is a place they can never return to again.

A home of one's own, on the other hand…

Don't let this be me in sixty years' time.

They'd been reminded of the old man for a reason. But perhaps that reason had everything to do with *life*, and nothing to do with *savings*: Bryann is a *they* now, but still very much *singular*, not plural.

They wonder what their rep would have to say on Cameron's charitable marketisation—they open Facefuck, and restart their chat.

Fancy half-a-lager?

The shrapnel in their pocket will stretch no further. The rep replies immediately.

Mine's a Stella.

He says, he'll raise them a pint; Bryann can pay him back later.

Render unto Caesar the things that are Caesar's.

Fuck the full hour; they log off the computer.

Render unto the Universe the things that are theirs.

Bryann steps from the establishment into unchartered constellations.

Author's Note

Glass House has been adapted from *Guerrilla Gardening*, performed at Pleasance Theatre (2002). *The Magic Machine* has been adapted from *I Love You but We Only Have Fourteen Minutes to Save the Earth*, performed at Soho Theatre (2012). *Submission* has been adapted from a play of the same name, written with support from Arts Council England (2004). An earlier draft of *Only Connect* was published in *Queerlings* magazine (2020). An earlier draft of *Going Up, Going Down* was published in the anthology *Mainstream* (Inkandescent, 2021). An earlier draft of *Fairy Story* was published in the journal *Untitled: Voices, Issue One* (2020). An earlier draft of *Beautiful Ones* was published in the anthology *Queer Life, Queer Love, Volume One* (Muswell Press, 2021).

Acknowledgements

Thank you to my publisher Justin David, and to my editor Bart Bennett—whose attention to detail enabled the manuscript to become the best possible version of itself.

To Leather Lane Writers, whose feedback helped shape every story—Katy Whitehead, Hugo Bennett, Neil Lawrence, Joshua Davis, Niki Seth-Smith, Alex Hopkins and Lisa Goldman.

To early readers of individual stories—Stephen Morris, Aliya Gulamani, Piero Toto, Polly Wiseman, Luke Buckingham.

To Allen Herron—for recording the cello part for the trailer.

To Jon Ransom, Iqbal Hussain and Kathy Hoyle—for giving their time, and their endorsement so generously.

To friends and family who've offered writing sanctuary—Lynn and Nick Wiseman in Lewes, Anthony Psaila in Margate, Tim Redfern in Rye, Mum and Dad in Brittany.

Also from Inkandescent

ONE LAST SONG
Nathan Evans

you're never too old to change your tune

A gentleman called Joan lands up in a care home like a colourful, combustible cocktail... ticking.

A gentleman called Jim doesn't know what's hit him... everything about his new next-door neighbour is triggering.

Battle begins. May the best man win. But beneath antics and antique armour plating, what are both hiding?

Maybe they've more than a wall in common?

Might they even be batting for the same team?

'An enchanting romance - funny, touching and inspiring'
STEPHEN FRY

Also from Inkandescent

THE DISAPPEARANCE BOY
NEIL BARTLETT

A new edition including a Foreword by the author, and an Afterword with
world famous illusionist, DERREN BROWN

1953. The backstreets of Brighton are buzzing with preparations for the
celebrations of the Coronation of Elizabeth II and, at the Grand Theatre,
illusionist Teddy Brookes is plotting something crowd-pleasing to crown
the occasion—with some assistance from glamorous Soho showgirl
Pamela Rose. What the audience can never see is that, hidden behind the
smoke and mirrors of his act, there is a whole world of secrets and lies…

And a disappearance boy.

In his acclaimed fourth novel, Neil Bartlett once again performs his
trademark trick of slipping into the hidden spaces of queer history and
bringing them vividly to life.

'Seductive, dark, theatrical and fascinating,
Bartlett's writing is spellbinding'
RUSSELL TOVEY

Also from Inkandescent

Tales of the Suburbs
Justin David

Part One of the Welston World Sagas
First Welston, then the World

As a boy growing up in the Black Country—drained grey by Mrs Thatcher's steely policies—Jamie dreams of escape to a magical metropolis where he can rub shoulders with the mythical creatures who inhabit the pages of his Smash Hits. Though his hometown is not without characters and Jamie's life not without dramas—courtesy of a cast of West Midlands divas led by his mother, Gloria. Her one-liners are as colourful as the mohair cardies she carries off with the panache of a television landlady.

We follow Jamie through secondary school, teenage troubles and away to art school; there he experiences the flush of first love with Billy, and the rush of the big city. But what then? Will he return to the safety of Welston, or risk everything on a new life in London?

These flamboyantly funny stories of self-discovery, set against the shifting social scenery of the 80s and 90s, are for everybody who's ever decided to be the person they are meant to be.

'Poignant storytelling, in which pithy dialogue and sharp characterisation make for compelling reading.'
PATRICIA ROUTLEDGE

Also from Inkandescent

THE PHARMACIST

Justin David

Part Three of the Welston World Sagas
when love is the drug

Twenty-four-year-old Billy is beautiful and sexy. Albert—The Pharmacist—is a compelling but damaged older man, and a veteran of London's late '90s club scene. After a chance meeting in the heart of the London's East End, Billy is seduced into the sphere of Albert. An unconventional friendship develops, fuelled by Albert's queer narratives and an endless supply of narcotics. Alive with the twilight times between day and night, consciousness and unconsciousness, the foundations of Billy's life begin to irrevocably shift and crack, as he fast-tracks toward manhood. This story of lust, love and loss is homoerotic bildungsroman at its finest.

'As lubricious as early Alan Hollinghurst,
The Pharmacist is a welcome reissue from Inkandescent, and the perfect
introduction to a singular voice in gay literature.'
THE TIMES LITERARY SUPPLEMENT

'At the heart of David's The Pharmacist is an oddly touching and bizarre
love story, a modern day Harold and Maude set in the drugged-up
world of pre-gentrification Shoreditch. The dialogue, especially,
bristles with glorious life.'
JONATHAN KEMP

Also from Inkandescent

MAINSTREAM
edited by Justin David & Nathan Evans

'A wonderful collection of fascinating stories by unique voices'.
KATHY BURKE

This collection brings thirty authors in from the mar-gins to occupy centre-page. Queer storytellers. Working class wordsmiths. Chroniclers of colour. Writers whose life experiences give unique perspectives on universal challenges, whose voices must be heard. And read.
Emerging writers are being placed alongside these established authors—

Bidisha, Elizabeth Baines, Gaylene Gould, Golnoosh Nour, Jonathan Kemp, Julia Bell, Keith Jarrett, Kerry Hudson, Kit de Waal, Juliet Jacques, Neil Bartlett, Neil McKenna, Padrika Tarrant, Paul McVeigh and Philip Ridley

'A riveting collection of stories, deftly articulated. Every voice entirely captivating: page to page, tale to tale. These are stories told with real heart from writers emerging from the margins in style.'
ASHLEY HICKSON-LOVENCE,
author of *The 392* and *Your Show*

Also from Inkandescent

I am not Raymond Wallace
Sam Kenyon

Manhattan, 1963: weeks before the assassination of President Kennedy, fresh-faced Raymond Wallace lands in the New York Times newsroom on a three-month bursary from Cambridge University. He soon discovers his elusive boss, Bukowski, is being covertly blackmailed by an estranged wife, and that he himself is to assist the straight-laced Doty on an article about the 'explosion of overt homosexuality' in the city. On an undercover assignment, a secret world is revealed to Raymond: a world in which he need no longer pretend to be something or someone he cannot be; a world in which he meets Joey.

Like so many men of his time and of his kind, Raymond faces a choice between conformity, courage and compartmentalisation. The decision he makes will ricochet destructively through lives and decades until—in another time, another city; in Paris, 2003—Raymond's son Joe finally meets Joey. And the healing begins.

'A sensual, moving story of masks and identities, across two continents and four decades... a strikingly confident debut novel.'
SAMUEL WEST

celebrating diversity

Inkandescent Publishing was created in 2016
by Justin David and Nathan Evans to shine a light on
diverse and distinctive voices.

Could you do one more Inkredible thing for us?
Sign up to our mailing list to stay informed
about future releases:

www.inkandescent.co.uk/sign-up

follow us on Facebook:

@InkandescentPublishing

on Twitter:

@InkandescentUK

on Threads:

@inkandescentuk

and on Instagram:

@inkandescentuk